I0541562

THE PRANK

A NOVEL

ADAM J BLACK

THE ARTLESS DODGES PRESS
WWW.THEARTLESSDODGESPRESS.COM
CLEVELAND, OHIO

The Prank
a novel by Adam Black
ISBN 0981993974
EAN-13 9780981993973
copyright © 2011 Artless Dodges, Inc.
Published by The Artless Dodges Press
Cleveland, Ohio
www.TheArtlessDodgesPress.com

Cover and title design by T. Maven
www.TrashMaven.WordPress.com

Author's Foreword:
A Comment on the Style and Content of THE PRANK

I wrote **THE PRANK** *with the idea that I was going to write a novel for the way we process information in the digital age. We don't read or watch most things from start to finish: the internet and the news sphere are so densely crowded that we tend to cherry pick our way through news shows or news articles (or blog posts, or Facebook news feeds) to find what is relevant to us. When we do find something that sparks our interest we don't stop and consider it more carefully: rather we continue to scan, constructing the narrative for ourselves out of the bits of information that we discover across a spectrum of media. We have all become experts at mining what is relevant from an overwhelming environment, and ignoring everything else: effectively "channel surfing" our way through the world.*

I wanted to write a novel in this style (at least in part) because I harbor a dark suspicion that this phenomenon is rapidly making conventional narrative irrelevant. I say this because in my own life I have found myself less and less inclined toward narrative: it lacks the irresistible "treasure hunt" quality of googling for threads of information, of flipping from one twenty-four-hour news network to another, titillated always by the thought that someone may have some exclusive breaking insight. What can narrative offer to match the thrill of this nearly effortless intermittent reward?

The irony, of course, is that ninety percent of what we discover when we are searching for information and constructing our narrative is redundant: the same information is returned in our searches or rebroadcast on our news networks with slightly different wording or a slightly different preamble; the mass of stimuli through which we find ourselves constantly wading is composed of innumerable reiterations and duplications. This only reaffirms the apparatus and deepens the problem: we <u>need</u> to channel surf to avoid reading what we've already read, hearing what we've already heard, wasting our time.

Wasting our time. It's what we're all trying to avoid. Of course on some level we all realize that the only way to avoid wasting our time would be to do something else and then return to the television, computer, etc., after enough time has elapsed for new information to surface. Strangely, we often do not. Again, we are titillated by the possibility that some new pertinent detail may be only second away...

THE PRANK *is a novel about the tendency for any news story involving a cute child or a reprehensible parent to become a media feeding frenzy, about the incredible communicative power of the internet, about the* *speed at which a fabricated happening can cross the threshold into accepted truth. But it is also about us as consumers of narrative: about how the digital revolution has changed the way we process information. My hope is that as you are reading you will find yourself scanning, skipping, dismissing, and cherry-picking: pay attention to these moments. This is your brain doing something remarkable, something profoundly post-modern, something perhaps not altogether benign.*

- A. B.

"And now, tonight's top story..."

And now reports coming in...

... And thank you Doug we will return to that story in a moment but right now reports coming in of troubling news tonight out of the flooded town of Gill Falls, Missouri, where an experimental watercraft which was designed by one of the residents has been carried away by the floodwaters and is currently on a direct course toward the Gill Falls Waterfall less than five miles downstream. The inventor of this craft, Mr. Frank Nevis, says that he is he is unable to locate his six-year-old daughter Melissa, and fears that she may have been hiding in the watercraft when the flooding started. I believe we have some video of Mr. Nevis...

...She was right there next to me one second and then I turned around to help my wife get up into the rescue boat with the other kids and when I turned around she was gone just like that, I went back to look for her and I saw the boat floating away she doesn't know how to steer oh God...

...Very disturbing indeed here we have a picture of Melissa Nevis, this picture taken earlier this year at Gill Falls Elementary School, where Miss Nevis is a student. Now at this time Search and Rescue crews are unable to reach the craft, which is traveling very swiftly towards the Gill Falls Waterfall. We are being told that there simply aren't enough Search and Rescue personnel to spare a boat for a rescue attempt, all available boats are being used for evacuation efforts. Fire Chief Bill Brixley had this to say...

...At this point it is unfeasible to get a boat out on the river. Right now we're able to maneuver within the town limits, because the banks create a buffer between the current and the floodwater. Once a craft is out on the river there is almost no controlling it...

The Gill Falls Fire Chief Bill Brixley saying that a rescue of the experimental craft is not possible at this point. We will have more on this story as it develops but right now our own Chris Firth on the scene in Gill Falls Chris I wonder if you can give us some sense of the pace and the volume that the river is flowing at, and just how serious this situation is for uh, for anyone in any sort of craft out on the water.

...Certainly Christy well the situation is certainly very severe for anyone out on the river at this point storm waters have obviously just completely inundated this whole area, the river is flowing over its banks I don't know if you can see behind me here but that stand of trees is the riverbank, and as you can see the bank is completely submerged, you wouldn't even know that it was ever there, so certainly we are talking about a tremendous volume of water, a tremendous amount of flooding and damage, and a tremendous danger to anyone who can't get up to higher ground...

@TooCool4School

Some cute, blond, white girl is in a boat heading for a waterfall. Can't wait to see the news media lose their shit. *10 minute ago*

@ReaderGrl03

What is happening in Gill Falls is just so sad... You would think we would learn from Katrina... Those who don't learn from their mistakes are condemned to repeat them. *7 minutes ago*

@DaQueenLives

please please please Jesus please God please save Melissa Nevis!!!!!! *7 minutes ago*

@INDIAnaJONES

nothing i like better than a news panic involving a helpless white female... wonder how many black children got washed away in new orleans... be proud of yourselves america *5 minutes ago*

@DaQueenLives

@INDIAnaJONES how can you even say that it's a little girl?!?!?!? Your really sick seek help *4 minutes ago*

@TinaNiceNotMean

ohmygosh! Melissa Nevis u r in are prayers! Repost if you believe in miracles! *2 minutes ago*

@WorldWideNewsNetwork

Breaking news in Melissa Nevis story live streaming at www.WWNN.com *1 minute ago*

@*MyNews16*
Breaking news on the Melissa Nevis story see more at www.mynews16.com *1 minute ago*

@*WeatherMan15*
With the amount of water going down that river it's going to be impossible to retrieve that boat... How about we spend our time and energy focusing on saving the people who can be saved *1 minute ago*

@*CatGirlUSA*
ohmygosh! Melissa Nevis u r in are prayers! Repost if you believe in miracles! *0 minutes ago*

@*Jeep365*
Melissa Nevis u r in are prayers! Repost if you believe in miracles! *0 minutes ago*

@*JulieB123*
Melissa Nevis u r in are prayers! Repost if you believe in miracles! *0 minutes ago*

@*GTOGuy17*
Who the f#ck is Melissa Nevis? *O minutes ago.*

...Sorry to interrupt you Bill but we have some breaking news now coming in from the scene of the terrible flooding in Gill Falls where residents and residents of other nearby towns have joined together and are going to try to bring that experimental vessel that's the vessel that may contain Melissa Nevis, that experimental vessel that her father Frank Nevis was building in the garage of the family's home, they're going to try to bring it to shore, let's go live right now to Phil Mitchell on the scene with Gill Falls Fire Chief Bill Brixley, Phil?

Thank you Melanie I'm here with Gill Falls Fire Chief Bill Brixley Chief could you tell us just briefly because I know you've got to go your efforts are needed elsewhere but if you could just tell us briefly what the residents are doing to try to bring this little girl safely to shore.

Ah sure so a half mile upstream of the falls is an overlook bridge and the idea is that we're going to lower a series of loops of ropes over the side of the bridge the entire width of the river which is going to form a sort of net apparatus and that when the vessel comes through that it's going to become entangled in those ropes and from there we're going to be able to pull it ashore.

Terrific and you told me earlier that this idea is entirely the work of the citizens, that the Search and Rescue crews already had their hands full and that the people said we want to do this, we *can* do this, and they got together and came up with a plan, really under the gun.

That's right we had already made the decision that for the safety of the crews working out here no rescue was going to be attempted... Uh... Their job is to help as many people as possible and in order to do that they have to make sure that they don't put themselves in a situation where they themselves need rescuing, so for situations like this we have to make a call based on the greater need but the residents...

...That's what I was going to say it's really an incredible story the residents came up with and executed this plan without... pretty much without your knowledge is that right?

Yes that is right we told these people to stay away, to once they were evacuated to stay out of the way but they came down here on their own and...

Really really incredible stuff and I'm sorry to cut you off here Fire Chief Bill Brixley but I'm being told that the boat the experimental vessel is now coming around the bend before the bridge. And we can see here the vessel coming into view you should be able to see it on your screen. This is happening live.

Are you watching?

Are you watching the news right now? Oh my God you have to turn on the news right now. Ok well you know how there is all that flooding from those storms? They're trying to evacuate this town right now and there's this little girl in a boat and she's getting pulled downstream towards this waterfall, and all the townspeople are trying to rescue her. No they haven't done it yet. They're trying to catch her with a bunch of ropes. They're hanging ropes off of this bridge right above the waterfall. Ok no go and watch it and then call me back after.

And now we're going to go live to Chad Homnick who's on the scene in Gill Falls and Chad I understand that the boat is now...

Yes sorry to cut in on you Jill but as you can see behind me the boat is now coming right down to the bridge... and there it looks like they've managed to catch it with the first line... I... and there we can see that the boat, that experimental vessel designed by Frank Nevis the father of Melissa Nevis who authorities believe is in that vessel is now being snared by the lines and now you can see the townspeople are starting to drag it to shore, the residents of Gill Falls and some of the surrounding towns have all come out to attempt this daring rescue... Search and Rescue crews could not make an attempt to retrieve the vessel we spoke with Fire Chief Bill Brixley earlier and he explained that his team simply did not have the resources to spare, there are too many other folks in need of help and so those who had already been rescued got together and said we can do this.... Wait, something is... It looks like, if I can just see... Oh no... It looks like the ropes that were... Oh no oh God... Oh no

www.WWNN.com

Breaking News:

Daring Rescue Attempt on Flood-Swollen River - Live Streaming Video

Defense Secretary Warns of Possible Terrorist Threat - Streaming Video

Gas Prices Expected to Climb: Price by State

Politics:

The Breakdown: Commentator Jim Matheson Gives His Take on the Candidates

Campaign Spending Reform Bill Tabled

Sports:

Kurt Vargis: Who to Watch This season: Rookies to Root For

Gene Randolf: No Surprises Heading into the Eastern Conference Finals

Entertainment:

Breakup to Makeup: A Look Back at the New Looks of the Recently Dumped

RLTV Greenlights New Reality Show "Dumpster Kings"

Money:

Government Bonds or Government Bondage? Liquidity in the Modern Market

Know When to Hold 'Em: Some Stocks You Shouldn't Dump Just Yet

Top Searches:

Melissa Nevis

Melisa Nevis

Gill Falls Girl

Melissa Navis

Flood

Flood Rescue

Dumpster Kings

Gas Prices

Sponsored Links:

Seasonal Allergy Sufferers: find fast relief this allergy season with Allergone, from the makers of NasaWell. www.Allergone.com

Live and Breaking from Gill Falls

...Once again if you're just joining us the rescue attempt on that experimental vessel that authorities believe contained six-year-old Melissa Nevis has failed... Here you can see in this video everything was going according to plan and then what happened apparently is that the current was too strong and it literally pulled the ropes from the rescuers' grasp, they had to let go or risk getting pulled over the railing and then you can see just for a moment the vessel gets hung up on one of the bridge's supports before the rushing floodwaters carry it over the edge of the waterfall. Now there has been no word as to the fate of that vessel or of Melissa Nevis who once again authorities believe was inside the vessel at the time of its... uh... at the time that it was carried over the falls... We take you now to Greg Davies who is on the scene in Gill Falls Greg if you could just give us a sense or give us your sense rather of the situation there.

Thank you Dave as you said the rescuers simply could not hold onto the ropes any longer, I spoke with one woman whose hands were burned by the ropes and there was a report that another man may have broken some fingers but anyway a very, very sad moment here in Gill

Falls as rescuers were unable to stop that vessel from being taken over the waterfall... It just goes to show you the sheer power of nature... And...

...Yes and we can see behind you the water seems even higher than it was just thirty minutes ago when this broadcast began.

...That's right Dave as you can see behind me the water has climbed several feet in fact in the few hours that we have been out here... The Search and Rescue crews are telling me that they expect even more water to be coming through as we get further on into the evening and on through the night as the runoff continues to come down the valley... Yet another reason why the rescue crews simply could not spare any personnel for this rescue attempt they are truly under the gun here, trying to make sure everyone is out before the situation here gets any worse.

And we will be checking back with Greg as this story continues to develop but I wonder if you would Greg or if you know if you would tell us what sort of efforts are underway to look for or recover the body of Melissa Nevis.

...Uh well I think everyone here is... No one has mentioned anything about that but my sense is that at this time there's nothing more that can be done, whatever happens it will have to happen after the floodwaters have receded, after it is safe to come back... Yes and I'm being told now by rescue personnel that we can't stay here any longer, we are going to have to move to higher ground, so I will have to hand it back to you Dave and we will talk to you again when... uh... when it is feasible to do so.

Greg Davies reporting there from Gill Falls and again very sad news as Melissa Nevis, the six-year-old resident of Gill Falls, has apparently been carried over the falls in that vessel the vessel her father made in the garage of the family's home... Again very sad news and we will be bringing you more information as it is made available to us but right now all rescue and recovery efforts are being postponed until the floodwaters have receded and until it is safe for rescue workers to do so. When we come back, more on this developing story.

Jenny Miller wrote...

Jenny Miller created the Facebook group **One Million Prayers for Melissa Nevis.** *7 minutes ago.*

Jenny Miller wrote on the wall for the group **One Million Prayers for Melissa Nevis**: In this terrible time our thoughts and prayers are with the friends and family of Melissa Nevis. Melissa, know that you are in our hearts and that you are loved, that all of those who loved you and who you loved in life will see you soon. This is an open group. Invite your friends! Let's get one million members! *7 minutes ago.*

Greg Hill joined the group **One Million Prayers for Melissa Nevis.** *6 minutes ago.*

Billy Feagans joined the group **One Million Prayers for Melissa Nevis.** *6 minutes ago.*

Rita Forlani joined the group **One Million Prayers for Melissa Nevis.** *6 minutes ago.*

Rita Forlani wrote on the wall for the group **One Million Prayers for Melissa Nevis**: Melisa Nevis you are in our prayers! *6 minutes ago.*

David Green joined the group **One Million Prayers for Melissa Nevis.** *5 minutes ago.*

Dotty Long joined the group **One Million Prayers for Melissa Nevis.** *5 minutes ago.*

Vicki DePew joined the group **One Million Prayers for Melissa Nevis.** *5 minutes ago.*

Dotty Long wrote on the wall for the group **One Million Prayers for Melissa Nevis**: Believe in miracles and they can come true! Do not give up hope! Frank, we are praying for your daughter's safe return! *5 minutes ago.*

Gill Smith joined the group **One Million Prayers for Melissa Nevis.** *4 minutes ago.*

Derrick Mills joined the group **One Million Prayers for Melissa Nevis.** *4 minutes ago.*

Derrick Mills wrote on the wall for the group **One Million Prayers for Melissa Nevis**: I joined this group so that I could say that this is the stupidest shit ever you don't even know these people and even if you did, praying to an imaginary god isn't going to do anything she got carried over a FUCKING WATERFALL. *4 minutes ago.*

Gill Smith commented on Derrick Mills's post on the wall for the group **One Million Prayers for Melissa Nevis**: This is exactly why Facebook should have a dislike button. *3 minutes ago.*

Derrick Mills's post has been deleted by the Administrator. *3 minutes ago.*

Bill Roberts joined the group **One Million Prayers for Melissa Nevis.** *3 minutes ago.*

Mindy Roberts joined the group **One Million Prayers for Melissa Nevis.** *3 minutes ago.*

Dean Stanwick joined the group **One Million Prayers for Melissa Nevis.** *2 minutes ago.*

Bobby Ringwald joined the group **One Million Prayers for Melissa Nevis.** *2 minutes ago.*

Bobby Ringwald wrote on the wall for the group **One Million Prayers for Melissa Nevis**: LOL !! Me cant believe that you can see who is viewing your profile! I can see the TOP 10 people and I am really OPENMOUTHED that my EX is still checking my Pix and my Profile. You can also see WHO CHECKS YOUR PR0FILE here) *2 minutes ago.*

Craig Brown joined the group **One Million Prayers for Melissa Nevis.** *1 minute ago.*

Lorrie Mays joined the group **One Million Prayers for Melissa Nevis.** *1 minute ago.*

Heidi Rickleman joined the group **One Million Prayers for Melissa Nevis.** *1 minute ago.*

Heidi Rickleman wrote on the wall for the group **One Million Prayers for Melissa Nevis**: WE LOVE YOU MELISSA! YOU ARE IN OUR THOUGHTS AND PRAYERS! *0 minutes ago.*

The People of Gill Falls Need Your Help

Title: **The People of Gill Falls Need Your Help - Please Donate Today**

Uploaded by: FloodReliefAmerica *12 hours ago*

Duration: 2:30

1,354,678 views / 2,451 likes / 4 dislikes

Description: The town of Gill Falls, MO. was devastated by floodwaters. Flood Relief for America is on the scene, helping victims of this disaster. Donate today by visiting *www.FloodReliefAmerica.com*

Opening: fade up from black to a low-angle shot of the town after the flood waters have receded. Begin voiceover:

Voiceover (Man): My grandfather moved to this town after the first World War. He and my grandmother raised my dad and my aunts and uncles right here. I went over to look at their house after they let us come back and it's just *gone.*

Smash cut to black, fade in on shot of badly-damaged house with the word "*devastation*" superimposed in white. Begin voiceover:

Voiceover (Woman): (weeping) I don't know what we'll do. I just don't know what we'll do.

Smash cut to black, fade in on shot of badly-damaged commercial area with the word "*disaster*" superimposed in white. Begin voiceover:

Voiceover (Older Man): I've lived here all my life, thought I was going to live here the rest of my life, but. I guess Mother Nature had other ideas.

Fade to black. Superimpose text: *The town of Gill Falls, MO. was hit by a hundred-year flood. Houses that had stood for decades were washed away in a matter of hours.*

Cut to footage of floodwaters washing away houses.

Fade to black. Superimpose text: *For hundreds of residents, life will never be the same.*

Cut to footage of crying families, etc.

Fade to black. Superimpose text: *But now, there is hope.*

Cut to still images of water bottles being distributed, families laughing and playing at the shelter. Fade to shot of Professional Young Woman walking toward the camera through the flood-damaged town.

Professional Young Woman: In this time of crisis we at Flood Relief for America are asking you to donate now. Every dollar you send pays for lodging for one night for a displaced resident. Five dollars can feed a family of four for a day. Now is the time when your donation can be of the most use. Please, in this time of need, look into your heart. Click the link below or text the word DONATE to

1-800-4RELIEF. Each text will automatically donate ten dollars for families in need. [Professional Young Woman is joined by the residents of Gill Falls, who walk with her towards the camera.] To those from whom much was taken, much will be given.

Fade to black. Superimpose text: *www.FloodRelief America.com. Please donate today. Paid for by United Christian Charities, LLC.*

User Comments:

floods like this are caused by changing weather patterns due to mans stupid and greedy industrial practices... in the coming years we are going to see more and mroe floods like this... hurricanes, tornados, melting polar ice caps... WHEN ARE POLITICIANS GOING TO STOP THEIR PARTISAN BICKERING AND RECOGNIZE THAT WE ARE IN THE MIDDLE OF A CATASTROPHE?!?!
DEMIANJ *11 hours ago 110 likes 40 dislikes*

What happened in Gill Falls is just so sad. People's whole lives, washed away in a matter of hours. It makes you think.
GINNYFULLER *11 hours ago*

If you want to donate money to the flood victims of Gill Falls then DO NOT do it through this charity... the united christian charities have a WELL DOCU-MENTED history of misusing donations... they don't steal but when you give them money you don't know what they will do with it... unless you support everything they do and would be all right with YOUR MONEY setting up christian schools in Africa or sending missionaries to the south pacific then DO

NOT donate... There are other better charities with t r a n s p a r e n t   a i d   p r a c t i c e s . . .   v i s i t www.thetruthaboutcharities .com if you don't believe me
TURNER14 *10 hours ago 20 dislikes*

Does anyone know what happened to Melissa Nevis, the girl who was in that boat that went over the waterfall? Has there been any word from the rescue people or her family?
OLIVIAK *10 hours ago*

So sad. So very, very sad. "And the waters prevailed exceedingly upon the earth; and all the high hills, that were under the whole heaven, were covered." GEN 7:19
MARKG1956 *9 hours ago.*

@OLIVIAK: do a search for "Frank Nevis"... there is a video of him talking about the efforts to locate his daughter's body... So sad
GINNYFULLER *9 hours ago*

@GINNYFULLER: Thnx will do
OLIVIAK *9 hours ago*

A Father's Plea: Help Me Find My Daughter

Title: **A Father's Plea: Help Me Find My Daughter**
Uploaded by: FrankNevis *15 hours ago*
Duration: 0:45
1,688,342 views / 4,500 likes / 0 dislikes

Description: Cell phone video looking for my daughter thanx every1 for prayers and support GOD BLESS YOU

Frank Nevis: So you can see we're down by the river and I'm recording this on my cell phone so I apologize for the bad quality... The river is down quite a bit and we're... We're looking for any sign of... um... Any sign of the boat that my daughter was in... There's my wife Vicki... Hi Vic, say hi to everyone...

Victoria Nevis: Hi everyone.

Frank Nevis: We know that a lot of people are concerned for our daughter and we know that a lot of you have been praying for us and for her and we just want to say how much we appreciate that and we know that God hears all prayers He hears everyone's prayers and we just want you all to know that... that... that we haven't given up hope... Please everyone just keep praying for my little girl... Here you say something Vic

Victoria Nevis: Thank you all for keeping us in your prayers we're not going to give up

User Comments:
OHMYGOD this is just so sad
TAMMY1 *15 hours ago*

So sad
FLYGUY56 *15 hours ago*

CHEAPVIAGRALIPITORPRESCRIPTIONDRUGS
CLICKHEREwww.ghsierh.com
URFRIEND *15 hours ago*

Our thoughts and prayers are with you Frank and Victoria! Don't give up hope miracles are REAL! GOD is love!
HEDIED4U *14 hours ago*

FUCK TONIGHT!!!!! Meet hot local singles!!!! Our nationwide database will HOOK YOU UP!!!!! Click here: www.hdiwia.com
JCASHMONEY *14 hours ago*

WORK FROM HOME MAKE $500/HOUR FILLING OUT INTERNET SURVEYS EASY MONEY! www.MakeMeMoney.com
FREEMONEYGIVEAWAY *13 hours ago*

So sad
MIKER1243 *12 hours ago*

SO SO SAD!!!! OMG!!!!
MANDYBANDY *12 hours ago*

melissa nevis you are in our prayers
PHILRUP *11 hours ago*

Anyone else find the title of this video odd / misleading? I mean... did he title it himself? And he's not really pleading for help...?
GRADYV *11 hours ago 4 likes 35 dislikes*

@GRADYV: I'd like to see how you'd act in the same situation.
VICEROY9 *11 hours ago 5 likes 0 dislikes*

The Gill Falls Flood: In the Midst of Catastrophe, Courage

by Franz Gillmer, Staff Writer

Gill Falls, MO - As flood waters rose beneath them, two dozen residents of Gill Falls, MO. and the surrounding towns stood on the narrow bridge overlooking the Gill Falls Waterfall, waiting.

They were waiting for the experimental vessel in which Melissa Nevis, the six-year-old daughter of Frank and Victoria and the youngest of their five children, was said to be hiding. The Gill Falls Elementary School student had allegedly climbed onboard the vessel only moments before the swollen river pulled it from dry-dock in the family's garage, and carried it toward the fifty-five-foot drop just a few miles downstream.

"We were all in the kitchen," said Frank Nevis. "We were standing in about two feet of water, and the rescue boat was at the back door. I was helping the other kids in and I didn't see Melissa."

The six-year-old often hid in the boat when frightened, Nevis explained, adding, "I went out to see if that's where she'd hid, and right then I saw the river carrying it away."

The vessel was of Nevis's own design, and incorporated a fully-enclosed cabin. Because of this feature authorities and rescuers were unable to confirm that Melissa Nevis was in the vessel at the time of its unplanned launch. To her father, however, there seemed little doubt.

"She was always hiding in there when there was thunder or lightning," he said. "I just don't know where else she would have gone."

Recovery of the vessel was out of the question, explained Gill Falls Fire Chief Bill Brixley. "We simply didn't have the manpower to spare," he said. "And there seemed no viable strategy. The first rule of Search and Rescue is, never put yourself in a situation where you are going to need rescuing."

So, unbidden and against the advice of rescue crews, Melissa's friends and neighbors gathered on the bridge above the falls, praying for a miracle. Their plan was simple: by dangling loops of rope into the water, they would snare the vessel as it passed beneath the bridge, and then drag it to shore.

"I don't remember who came up with the plan," said Hal Levinworth, one of the townspeople who was on the bridge. "I just remember us all agreeing that it was the best option we had. We literally had no time to come up with another idea."

It was an idea that, for one hope-filled moment, seemed good enough.

"The boat came into view," recalls Levinworth, "and we all got a good grip on our lines. As it came under us it got caught on a couple of the loops, and so we all let go of our lines and held onto the ones that were caught. The ropes were all soaking wet, and nobody could hang on. The river was pulling like crazy, and then just like that we lost her."

In less than thirty seconds the boat was disentangled and out of sight, lost over the falls. But, say Melissa's parents, there is still reason to hope.

"I built that thing to be watertight all the way around," said Frank Nevis. "If it didn't hit anything on the way down it could still be intact. We're not ready to give up hope yet."

As of this writing the vessel has not been located. Until it is, the Nevis family takes comfort in the knowledge that when they needed help, their friends and neighbors did everything they could.

"That's just the way I was raised," said Deedee Richards, another resident who was on the bridge that day. "When people need help, you help them. We all have to look out for each other out here."

Franz Gillmer is a Staff Writer for the Miterville Post-Herald. This article is available online at www.Miterville PostHerald.com. Contact Franz directly at FranzGillmer @mitervillepostherald.com.

People are being killed! Is anyone listening?

www.FearBlog.org
Be afraid. Be very afraid.

Title: *don't go chasing waterfalls*
By: *dannydarko69*

An open letter to the people of Gill Falls: What the f%ck is wrong with you?!? Didn't you listen when the police told you to evacuate? Now we're supposed to feel sorry for you??? It's your own damn fault!!

I don't want to seem unsympathetic to the plight of people in the midst of a natural disaster but come on, seriously?!? The evacuation order went out TWO DAYS before the flood actually hit. That's plenty of time to leave. That's plenty of time to *PACK UP* and leave!!!!

So I turn on my TV and on EVERY FREAKING STATION there is coverage from the flood... HELLO? IS ANYBODY LISTENING? PEOPLE ARE BEING KILELD IN IRAQ AND AFGHANISTAN! WE ARE IN THE MIDDLE OF A FREAKING WAR PEOPLE! THERE ARE MUCH BIGGER THINGS AT STAKE!

To the Nevis family: sorry your daughter went over a waterfall. Maybe you should have paid better attention to where your kids were or maybe you should have LEFT WHEN THEY TOLD YOU TO LEAVE. Just saying.

The People of Gill Falls Need Your Help (NEW VER-SION)

Title: **The People of Gill Falls Need Your Help (NEW VERSION) - Please Donate Today**
Uploaded by: FloodReliefAmerica *3 hours ago*
Duration: 2:25
4,328 views / 111 likes / 25 dislikes
Description: During the flooding in the town of Gill Falls, MO. six-year-old Melissa Nevis was carried away by the rising river. Now her parents are asking for your help. Help the search for Melissa and donate today by visiting *www.FloodReliefAmerica.com*

Opening: fade up from black to a low-angle shot of the town after the floodwaters have receded. Begin voice-over:
Voiceover (Frank Nevis): I remember bringing her back here, back to our home, for the first time.

Smash cut to black, fade in on shot of badly-damaged house with the word "*devastation*" superimposed in white. Begin voiceover:

Voiceover (Victoria Nevis): (weeping) She was my little angel.

Smash cut to black, fade in on still image of Melissa Nevis with the word "*heartbreak*" superimposed in white. Fade to black. Superimpose text: *The town of Gill Falls, MO. was hit by a hundred-year flood. Houses that had stood for decades were washed away in a matter of hours. During the evacuation, six-year-old Melissa Nevis was carried away.*

Cut to footage of floodwaters washing away houses.

Fade to black. Superimpose text: *For hundreds of residents, life will never be the same.*

Cut to footage of crying families, etc.

Fade to black. Superimpose text: *But now, there is hope.*

Cut to still images of water bottles being distributed, families laughing and playing at the shelter. Fade to shot of Professional Young Woman walking toward the camera through the flood-damaged town.

Professional Young Woman: In this time of crisis we at Flood Relief for America are asking you to donate now. Every dollar you send pays for lodging for one night for a displaced resident. Five dollars can feed a family of four for a day. Now is the time when your donation can be of the most use. Please, in this time of need, look into your heart. Click the link below or text the word DONATE to 1-800-4RELIEF. Each text will automatically donate ten dollars for families in need. [Professional Young Woman is joined by the residents of Gill Falls, who walk with her towards the camera.] To those from whom much was taken, much will be given.

Fade to black. Superimpose text: *Flood Relief for America is committed to the task of locating Melissa Nevis and rebuilding Gill Falls. Visit www.FloodReliefAmerica .com for more information on how you can help. Please donate today. Paid for by United Christian Charities, LLC.*

User Comments:
HAHAHA they couldn't get that chick at the end to come back and film another segment? Here's to a totally phoned-in "please help" video.
BIGCLIFF7 *2 hours ago*

@BIGCLIFF7: don't you have some puppies to torture or something? Nice comment you sociopath piece of sh*t.
MORGAN4REAL *2 Hours ago 2 likes 0 dislikes*

These people are in desperate need it is such a sad story my cousin used to live in Gill Falls and she said that the Nevises are super nice people
BOBBYXYZ123 *2 hours ago*

@MORGAN4REAL: Don't get it twisted. I think it sucks what happened in Gill Falls. I'm just saying its totally crass to exploit it and slap together a video in 5 mintues
BIGCLIFF7 *1 hour ago 5 likes 0 dislikes*

...Thank you Phil and we'll have more on that story as it continues to develop. Well the search continues tonight in the area below the Gill Falls Waterfall for any sign of that experimental vessel containing what authorities fear will be the body of the so-called "Gill Falls Girl," six-year-old Melissa Nevis. Now we've been bringing you updates on this search as it has been going on... Jack Baker is on the scene there in Gill Falls Jack can you tell us what has happened since we spoke with you last?

Thank you Henry uh well as you can see behind me the Search and Rescue crews are using dogs to try and locate the missing girl these dogs are highly trained, um, they are specially trained to sniff out survivors in disasters like this one. I was speaking with one of the crew members earlier and he told me that one of these dogs can smell a person through two feet of rubble so everyone here is very optimistic that with the help of these rescue dogs they will find Melissa Nevis....

I see and have you heard anything is there any word as to what rescue crews are speculating might be Melissa's condition when they find her? We're talking about now three days since the flood waters receded five days since that vessel was seen going over the falls... Is there reason to, uh, to hope?

Well I spoke with Frank Nevis earlier and one of the things he said to me was that if Melissa was able to survive the initial fall that there are some supplies in the vessel itself, and Melissa would know how to get to them. Of course we don't know if she may be injured or in some other way compromised so time is of course of the essence.

Thanks Jack a very, very compelling story tonight as Search and Rescue crews continue to look for Melissa Nevis... Now we will continue to bring you updates all throughout our broadcast so please stay with us.

Hayden Green wrote...

Hayden Green joined the group **One Million Prayers for Melissa Nevis.** *21 minutes ago.*

Hayden Green wrote on the wall for the group **One Million Prayers for Melissa Nevis:** R.I.P Melissa Nevis... Heaven has one more angel *21 minutes ago.*

Carrie Brown wrote on the wall for the group **One Million Prayers for Melissa Nevis:** wait, she's dead? *20 minutes ago*

Dave Bishop wrote on the wall for the group **One Million Prayers for Melissa Nevis:** R.I.P Melissa Nevis *19 minutes ago*

Vicky McVie wrote on the wall for the group **One Million Prayers for Melissa Nevis:** R.I.P Melissa Nevis *19 minutes ago*

Hillary Noonan wrote on the wall for the group **One Million Prayers for Melissa Nevis:** No wait seriously you guys where did you hear that she died? *18 minutes ago*

Vicky McVie wrote on the wall for the group **One Million Prayers for Melissa Nevis:** www.Gary CountyNews.com/Melissa_Nevis_Body_Found.html *17 minutes ago*

Karen Filmore wrote on the wall for the group **One Million Prayers for Melissa Nevis:** R.I.P Melissa Nevis heaven has one more angel *17 minutes ago*

Melissa Nevis Body Found
by Hillary Serta, Staff Writer
*www.GaryCountyNews.com/Melissa_Nevis_Body_Found.
html*

Gill Falls, MO. - After five long days of worrying and wondering, the Nevis family's wait has come to an end.

At 11:30 PM specially trained Search and Rescue dogs led responders to a densely-wooded area beneath the Gill Falls Waterfall. There crews discovered the wreckage of Frank Nevis' experimental watercraft and the body of six-year-old Melissa Nevis.

At this time there has been no comment as to the cause of death, although initial reports from the crash site indicate that the impact was severe and most likely responsible.

As of this writing no new comment has been released by the Nevis family.

Hillary Serta is a Staff Writer for the Gary County News. Contact her directly at HSerta@GaryCountyNews.com.

So wait... She's dead?

@BossONova90
RIP Melissa Nevis... www.GaryCountyNews. com/Melissa_Nevis_Body_Found.html *4 minutes ago*

@PHILipino69
So wait... She's dead? We're 100% on this? *3 minutes ago*

@TOMMYBAHAMA98
I could only find one article that said it but now the other news sites are picking up on it *2 minutes ago*

@MelBaker56
Shes dead shes not shes dead shes not make up your mind america *2 minutes ago*

@DeeDeeSweatPea
So sad... Frank and Victoria Nevis you are in our prayers *1 minute ago*

@SurferSean
So this has been confirmed? *1 minute ago*

@TammyWhammy23
So so sad... RIP Melissa Nevis *0 minutes ago*

@MistakenID
RIP Melissa Nevis *0 minutes ago*

www.WWNN.com/Melissa_Nevis_Body_Found.html

Gill Falls, MO. - After five long days of worrying and wondering, the Nevis family's wait has come to an end.

At 11:30 PM specially trained Search and Rescue dogs led responders to a densely-wooded area beneath the

Gill Falls Waterfall. There crews discovered the wreckage of Frank Nevis' experimental watercraft and the body of six-year-old Melissa Nevis.

At this time there has been no comment as to the cause of death, although initial reports from the crash site indicate that the impact was severe and most likely responsible.

As of this writing no new comment has been released by the Nevis family.

by Hillary Serta, Staff Writer for the Gary County News. Source: www.GaryCountyNews.com/Melissa_Nevis_Body _Found.html

And now unconfirmed reports...

...Breaking news out of Gill Falls tonight as the search for Melissa Nevis is finally over. With the help of specially-trained dogs rescue workers were able to locate the site where that experimental vessel came crashing down after floodwaters forced it over the waterfall late last Saturday afternoon. Now according to reports Melissa Nevis was inside the vessel as expected but did not survive the impact. Tonight our thoughts and prayers are with the Nevis family and we will continue to bring you more on this story as it comes to us.

Gill Falls, MO. - After five long days of worrying and wondering, the Nevis family's wait has come to an end.

At 11:30 PM specially trained Search and Rescue dogs led responders to a densely-wooded area beneath the Gill Falls Waterfall. There crews discovered the wreckage of Frank Nevis' experimental watercraft and the body of six-year-old Melissa Nevis.

At this time there has been no comment as to the cause of death, although initial reports from the crash site indicate that the impact was severe and most likely responsible.

As of this writing no new comment has been released by the Nevis family.

by Hillary Serta, Staff Writer for the Gary County News. Source: www.GaryCountyNews.com/Melissa_Nevis_Body _Found.html

---

Gill Falls, MO. - After five long days of worrying and wondering, the Nevis family's wait has come to an end.

At 11:30 PM specially trained Search and Rescue dogs led responders to a densely-wooded area beneath the Gill Falls Waterfall. There crews discovered the wreckage of Frank Nevis' experimental watercraft and the body of six-year-old Melissa Nevis.

At this time there has been no comment as to the cause of death, although initial reports from the crash site indicate that the impact was severe and most likely responsible.

As of this writing no new comment has been released by the Nevis family.

by Hillary Serta, Staff Writer for the Gary County News. Source: www.GaryCountyNews.com/Melissa_Nevis_Body _Found.html

Heartbreaking news tonight...

...Well heartbreaking news tonight out of Gill Falls as we are being told that the body of six-year-old Melissa Nevis has been recovered by rescuers. Viewers will recall that Melissa Nevis climbed aboard her father's experimental boat which was being stored in the garage of the family's home, and was almost immediately carried away by the rising floodwaters late last Saturday. To Frank and Victoria Nevis from all of us here at the National News Network, our deepest sympathies.

www.WorldNewsCorp.com/Melissa_Nevis_Body_Found. html

Gill Falls, MO. - After five long days of worrying and wondering, the Nevis family's wait has come to an end.

At 11:30 PM specially trained Search and Rescue dogs led responders to a densely-wooded area beneath the Gill Falls Waterfall. There crews discovered the wreckage of Frank Nevis' experimental watercraft and the body of six-year-old Melissa Nevis.

At this time there has been no comment as to the cause of death, although initial reports from the crash site indicate that the impact was severe and most likely responsible.

As of this writing no new comment has been released by the Nevis family.

by Hillary Serta, Staff Writer for the Gary County News. Source: www.GaryCountyNews.com/Melissa_Nevis_Body _Found.html

www.GaryCountyNews.com/Melissa_Nevis_Body_Foun d.html

The page cannot be found.

The page you are looking for might have been removed, had its name changed, or is temporarily unavailable.

Please try the following:
- If you typed the address into the Address bar, make sure that it is spelled correctly.
- Open the http://www.GaryCountyNews.com home page, and look for links to the information you want.
- Click the Back button to try another link.
- Click Search to look for information on the Internet.

HTTP 404 - File not found

www.GaryCountyNews.com/Melissa_Nevis_Body_Foun d.html

---

by Hal Binder, Editor-in-Chief

A regrettable error has come to my attention.

In the online edition of our publication a story was released stating that the body of Melissa Nevis had been recovered by rescuers. This was done in error. At this time the Gary County News has no information to verify this report.

In our haste to cover what we took to be a breaking development we failed in our journalistic responsibilities. We would like to take this opportunity to apologize to our readers, as well as to the family of Melissa Nevis.

Hal Binder is the Editor-in-Chief of the Gary County News. Contact him directly at HBinder@GaryCounty News.com.

Melissa Nevis FOUND!!!! YOU HAVE TO SEE THIS!!!!

Title: **Melissa Nevis has been found!!!!!**
Uploaded by: ViceRoy134 *5 hours ago*
Duration: 4:13
6,904 views / 154 likes / 325 dislikes
Description: During the flooding in the town of Gill Falls, MO. six-year-old Melissa Nevis was carried away by the rising river. Now the boat she was in has been found...

Scene: Two teenage boys walking through the woods. Sound of water in the distance.

1st Teenage Boy: We've looked everywhere, we're never going to find her.

2nd Teenage Boy: Dude just shut up we've got... No we're looking for Melissa Nevis stop being such a tool (laughs).

1st Teenage Boy: I'm not being a tool I'm just saying we're never going to find her.

3rd Teenage Boy (camera operator): You guys just shut up we're totally going to find her just shut up.

Scene: The Teenage Boys enter a clearing, in the center of which is an overturned rowboat.

1st Teenage Boy: Oh my God I think we've found Melissa Nevis.

2nd Teenage Boy: No way!

The boys run over and lift the rowboat. Inside is a girl of indeterminate preteen age. She appears to be asleep.

1st Teenage Boy: It's her! Is she alive?

3rd Teenage Boy (camera operator): I don't know man shake her wake her up.

2nd Teenage Boy: (Takes the girl by the shoulders, and begin to shake her) Hey! Are you alive? Wake up!

Girl: (waking up) Where am I?

2nd Teenage Boy: You're in the woods. You went over a waterfall. We found you.

1st Teenage Boy: We found her, we totally found her!

Scene: The Teenage boys and the preteen girl are walking alongside a river.

Girl: I'm hungry. I'm thirsty. I have to go to the bathroom. How long is it going to take until we get there? I don't think you guys know where you're going.

1st Teenage Boy: I had no idea she was going to be so annoying.

2nd Teenage Boy: I know I'm about to freaking lose my mind.

Girl: What are your names? Where do you go to school? Do you want to hear about my best friend Jessica? La la la la la la

1st and 2nd Teenage Boys: (together) That's it!

The boys take the girl by the arms and throw her into the river. Cut to stock footage of Niagara Falls, over-dubbed with the sound of the girl screaming.

Teenage Boys: (together, overdubbed) The end!

User Comments:
This video is in really really REALLY bad taste.
FOREVRLUV *5 hours ago 42 likes 0 dislikes*

@FOREVRLUV: I disagree. This video is an insult to bad taste.
MILES2GO *5 hours ago 47 likes 0 dislikes*

I hate to admit it, but I sort of agree... This whole Melissa Nevis thing is getting SUPER annoying... Would love to turn on the TV and hear about anything else...
SEXYSARAH1 *4 hours ago 3 likes 7 dislikes*

@SEXYSARAH: WORD
HURLEYGURLY *4 hours ago*

Tom Henry: Well they haven't found their daughter but what they have found is an outpouring of support from the many people their story has touched. In Gill Falls, Missouri, Greg Bradley has the story.

Greg Bradley: I'm standing in what used to be the Nevis family's front yard. Here Melissa Nevis played with her brothers and sisters and the other neighborhood children. But as you can see, there are no children playing in the yards along this street. That's because one week ago floodwaters brought devastation to this quiet town, leaving heartbreak and ruin in their wake and changing life for these residents forever.

But now, even in the midst of this devastation, there is hope.

Victoria Nevis: We are just so touched and so blessed.

Greg Bradley: This is Victoria Nevis. For many residents the damage from this event can be measured in possessions lost or destroyed but for Victoria and her family the floodwaters took something much more precious: they took Victoria's six-year-old daughter, Melissa.

Paul Brown: The response has just been incredible.

Greg Bradley: This is Paul Brown. Paul is the chief outreach officer for Flood Relief for America, one of the many charities that has been working to raise money for the monumental task of rebuilding the town that faces the residents of Gill Falls. He says that in this case, the response has been surprising.

Paul Brown: I've been working with FRA for twelve years and I have never seen a response like this. The generosity, the outpouring of support, the number of people who are driving out on the weekends to help, just showing up and saying, you know, put me to work... I've never seen anything like it.

Greg Bradley: The difference, Paul says, is six-year-old Melissa Nevis.

Paul Brown: People hear the story and they want to help. They want to give. They want to do what they can.

Greg Bradley: For Victoria Nevis and her family, the response has been nothing short of a miracle.

Victoria Nevis: The love that people have for Melissa, people who didn't know her, people who have never met her, are coming up to me everyday and telling me that they're praying for her, praying for all of us. It's amazing. It's wonderful.

Greg Bradley: Even though the response has been tremendous, Paul Brown is quick to point out that the recovery is far from complete, and there is still a lot of work to be done.

Paul Brown: Come out. Drive out on a weekend. Bring your family, we'll put you to work. This is what America is. This is what Americans do. They help each other.

Greg Bradley: Anyone looking for more information on how they can help can visit Flood Relief America dot com or the Melissa Nevis Fund dot com that is a fund set up by the members of Melissa's church and that money will go directly to relief efforts.

Tom Henry: Greg Bradley there with a special report from Gill Falls and the ongoing situation there. Now at this time Melissa Nevis's body has still not been recovered, and we are being told that nothing was found in the search of the area below the waterfall and so the next step is to send divers into the river itself but they, uh, we are being told that the water volume has to drop before it is safe for divers to make any attempt.

You Searched for: Frank Nevis
789,001 Results
Search results returned in .11 Seconds

Frank Nevis is on Facebook!
Frank Nevis is on Facebook. Join Facebook to connect with **Frank Nevis** and others you may know. Facebook gives people the power to share and makes the world...
www.Facebook.com/people/franknevis.html - *see more results like this*

Frank Nevis profile LinkedIn
View the profiles of professionals named **Frank Nevis** on LinkedIn. There are 21 professionals named **Frank Nevis**, who use LinkedIn to exchange information...
www.linkedin.com/pub/dir/Frank/Nevis - *see more results like this*

Frank Nevis Online
Hello and welcome to FrankNevis.com, the place to find all the latest... **Frank Nevis**... home - inventions - videos - contact...
www.FrankNevis.com - *see more results like this*

Family Still Waiting...
The family is still waiting to hear... says **Frank Nevis**, the girl's father... Click to contact us... Follow us on Twitter
www.WorldNewsNetwork.com/flood_victim_family_still_waiting... - *see more results like this*

US Patent No. 6705687 Oscillating Blender
Oscillating blender. Patent No. 6705687. Issued to: **Frank Nevis**. Filed: October 16, 2001. PCT Filed: February 13, 2001 ...
www.bgmlegal.com/6705677.html - *see more results like this*

US Patent No. 6995749 Accordion Closet Organizer
Accordion closet organizer. Patent No. 6995749. Issued to: **Frank Nevis**. Filed: May 23, 2003. PCT Filed: September 24, 2003 ...
www.bgmlegal.com/6995749.html - *see more results like this*

Show Transcript: Pilot 67900-12
... **Frank Nevis**: Hi everyone! Welcome to... This transcript is the exclusive property of The Continental Cable Company and may not be reproduced....
www.DeadShows.com/reality/7593 - *see more results like this*

A WWNN Exclusive: America is Reaching Out
Tune in tonight to see an exclusive interview with **Frank** and Victoria **Nevis**, as they wait to hear news of their daughter Melissa... follow us on Twitter...
www.WWNN.com/exclusive/america_is_reaching_ou t.html - *see more results like this*

Page 1 - Next
Searches related to "Frank Nevis":
Frank Nevis Flood
Melissa Nevis
Gill Falls Girl

Flood Girl
Flood Family
Victoria Nevis

Search for "Frank Nevis" in:
Everything
Videos
News
Shopping
More

This Sunday's sermon will be given...

To Note:
This Sunday's sermon will be given by Associate Pastor Ralph Vickers. Head Pastor David Brennen will be in Gill Falls, ministering to those displaced by the recent flooding. Volunteers wishing to accompany Pastor Dave on his trip should contact him at DavidBrennen@NewLife Church.org. The bus will leave the Church parking lot at 12 AM Saturday morning and return at 9 PM Sunday night. Food, clothing, tools, and building material donations are being accepted in the Church office.

People don't know them like we know them.

Title: **Other Voices from Gill Falls**
Uploaded by: GTOGuy *7 hours ago*
Duration: 6:31
6,980 views / 253 likes / 171 dislikes

Description: What some of the other residents of Gill Falls have to say about the flood and the Nevis family.

Scene: *The front yard of a house. A middle-aged man is raking garbage off of the muddy ground.*

Camera Operator: So what would you say to them, if you could say anything? What would you tell the news people about the Nevis family? Or what would you say to the Nevis family?

Middle-Aged Man: I would say stop trying to make this all about yourselves. People in this town have put up with your showboating and your grandstanding for long enough. People don't know. People don't know them like we know them.

Scene: *Garage interior. A young couple is sitting in a pair of lawn chairs.*

Camera Operator: What do you think people should know about the Nevis family, that they might not be getting from watching the news?

Young Woman: I just think that... I just think that everybody here is suffering, you know. Everyone here has lost their entire lives. I mean, look at this. We lost... we lost everything, you know.

Young Man: I think what people don't know is that they do this with everything that happens here. Everything, they always find a way to make it all about them.

Young Woman: Yeah. Yeah. Or... well at least Frank does. I've talked to Victoria. Victoria's nice. Frank... Frank is another story altogether.

Young Man: It's like, I'm really sorry that you never got famous. I really am. I really wish that he was a big success, because then he would live in California and the Californians would have to put up with him.

Both laugh.

Scene: *Interior of a school gymnasium, set up as a temporary shelter. A young woman sits on a cot with a toddler in her lap.*

Camera Operator: Do you think there's anything that people should know about the Nevis family? I mean is there anything that they're not getting from all of the news stories that maybe they should know before they send money or whatever, drive up here to help?

Young Woman: (*Shakes her head*) I don't know. I have to live here, you know? (*Laughs*) I don't want to say anything that might come back to haunt me.

Camera Operator: People, some of the people I've been talking to, just feel like the people who are coming up or who are sending money are being misled, that somebody really ought to tell them what it's like living here with them.

Young Woman: I don't know. I mean, I don't think it's fair to judge them. Frank... They just want different things than what most of the people in this town want, you know? They're just out of place. That's what I'll say: they're not bad, they're just out of place here. That work for you?

Camera Operator: Sure. Thanks.

Scene: *Interior of commercial kitchen. A middle-aged man is washing dishes in the sink.*

Camera Operator: I'm trying to put together a little video portrait of the Nevis family from some of their neighbors, the people who really know them. A lot of people think the news shows aren't really giving a clear idea of what they're like.

Middle-Aged Man: Hmmm.

Camera Operator: I was wondering if you had anything to say.

Middle-Aged Man: About Frank Nevis? Me? Naw. (*Laughs*)

Camera Operator: No?

Middle-Aged Man: No. Well... No, I really shouldn't.

Camera Operator: What if...

Middle-Aged Man: Well maybe I'll just say that... You didn't see them out there, did you?

Camera Operator: No, they're not out there.

Middle-Aged Man: No they most certainly are not, because right now they're having dinner with the Governor.

Camera Operator: Is that right?

Middle-Aged Man: (*Nods*) That's right.

Camera Operator: Well, I mean....

Middle-Aged Man: I know, I know. So what? You're right. They're America's favorite flood victim family, it's not their fault. I mean, they probably didn't *mean* to become famous, using this tragedy that, I might add, has had an impact on every single person in this building, in this town... They probably didn't *mean* to use it for their own personal gain... No, never mind. I'm probably just reading too much into it.

Scene: Slow pan across a row of damaged houses. The camera comes to rest on one in the series, around which a dozen people are working.

Camera Operator: (*Approaches one woman who is standing near the perimeter*) Excuse me, could you tell me what's going on here?

Woman: We're working on trying to fix up some of the flood damage on the Nevis house. Do you know the Nevis family?

Camera Operator: Sure, yeah, so where did you all come from?

Woman: Well my family and I came down with some people from our church group but there are a couple of other church groups working here too.

Camera Operator: Uh-huh. I see a lot of people working on this house but there are all of these other houses that seem like they got just as messed up from the flood. Couldn't some of these people be working on some of these other houses?

Woman: I don't know about that I just came down... The Pastor at our church spoke with Frank Nevis and we were all set to work on the Nevis house. I don't know anything about any of these other ones.

User Comments:

Yes it is sad the way that the news media make celebrities of the victims of tragedies but it isn't their fault that ppl want to help them
FLYGIRL2 *5 hours ago 2 likes 3 dislikes*

I think the point is that the nevis family could be doing a lot more to help everyone else in the town... yes it isn't their fault that people want to help them but it is their fault if they don't share the luv
MISTERTWISTER *5 hours ago 5 likes 0 dislikes*

THIS VIDEO IS AN EXPLOITIVE PIECE OF SHIT
DIESALDAVE45 *4 hours ago 1 likes 4 dislikes*

bigmusclegains i cant believe it you guys so much better than any other product on the market!!!! big muscle gains added 20lb to my max in 3 days!!!! click

here check it out don't get left behind www.sjhbadsk.
com
WEIGHTROOMWILLY *4 hours ago*

OMG why would you pick on these people after
they've been through such a horrible tragedy!?!
BECKYFROMCINCI *4 hours ago*

Video that came to us only moments ago...

We apologize for the interruption and will return you
to your regularly scheduled programing in just a moment
but breaking news out of Gill Falls... uh, this video which
came to us only moments ago rescuers have located that
experimental watercraft in which six-year-old Melissa
Nevis was hiding when floodwaters carried it from the
garage of the family's home... Here it is we have video
from only moments ago and you can see the vessel being
pulled from the river just a few hundred yards, I'm being
told, downstream from the waterfall... As you can see
damage appears to be substantial no word as of yet
whether Melissa Nevis is inside but for the Nevis family,
after so many days of waiting and wondering, I'm certain
that this is a... uh, this is a disturbing and unwelcome
sight... Again it has been now seven days since the flooding which forced residents of Gill Falls and some of the
surrounding communities to evacuate their homes, and it
was seven days ago that Melissa Nevis, the craft carrying
Melissa Nevis, was carried over the waterfall... Rescuers
had been unable to search the river due to the... to the violent... uh, and here yes now we're seeing they've got the
vessel up on shore... uh, rescuers were unable to search

☂ *47*

the river due to the increased water volume and the violent current... And, uh, we will, uh, bring you more of that video at five o'clock during the five o'clock news hour, once again the vessel in which Melissa Nevis was a passenger has been recovered from the river... We will bring you... uh, we will bring you more as it comes to us.

We now go live to Lou Baker, on the scene in Gill Falls.

...More news out of Gill Falls tonight as the vessel in which Melissa Nevis was carried over the Gill Falls Waterfall during last week's flooding has been recovered from the river... We now go live to Lou Baker, on the scene in Gill Falls. Lou?

Thank you Carol well more heartbreak in Gill Falls tonight as the vessel that carried Melissa Nevis over the waterfall you see behind me has been recovered from the river... Now I am being told by the Search and Rescue crews that Melissa Nevis' body is not inside but as you may be able to see... They've got the scene pretty well roped off here but as you may be able to see there is a substantial hole in the side of the boat and rescuers are speculating that perhaps with the current her body might have been pulled from the wreck at some point during the seven days between when she went over the falls and the recovery of the wreck only... uh, only a few short hours ago.

Thank you Lou, Lou Baker on the ground in Gill Falls. Tell me Lou, have Melissa's parents commented on the recovery or... uh, has there been any indication of what their thoughts are at this time?

Uh, as of yet they have not, Carol... A representative for the family gave a statement when the boat was pulled from the water indicating that the Nevis family, that they were not going to give up hope that their daughter might still... might make it back home safe to them.

Thank you, Lou. Once again the vessel in which Melissa Nevis was carried over the Gill Falls Waterfall a full seven days ago has been recovered, although her body has not. Now we will have more for you on this developing story as more information comes to us.

A message to Melissa Nevis from your family

Title: **Melissa We Love You**
Uploaded by: FrankNevis *20 minutes ago*
Duration: 1:05
113 views / 35 likes / 5 dislikes
Description: A message to Melissa Nevis from your family

Frank Nevis: Hey Melissa, we're all here, say hi everybody.

Nevis Children: (*together, waving*) Hi Melissa

Frank Nevis: (*to Victoria Nevis*) Say hi to Melissa baby.

Victoria Nevis: Hi honey

Frank Nevis: We just wanted to tell you that we love you and that... Everything happens for a reason and we know God and Jesus are going to look out for you and you're going to... Going to be all right no matter what happens... Right kids?

Nevis Children: (*together, nodding*) uh-huh.

Frank Nevis: And we just want you to know that we're not giving up, we're praying all the time and we know that... know that you're going to come back to us. Right, babe?

Victoria Nevis: Right. We love you honey. We're going to see you really soon, ok?

Frank Nevis: Ok. All right say goodbye, kids. Tell Melissa you love her.

Nevis Children: (*together, waving*) Bye Melissa... Love you.

Frank Nevis: I love you honey. We'll all be together again really soon.

User Comments:
Seriously? Come on now...
GRIZZLYBR4 *19 minutes ago*

This is SO SAD
CoyoteUgly789 *19 mintues ago*

We are praying for you Frank and Victoria you are right everything DOES happen for a reason God has a plan for all of us never loose faith
AXEMANCOMETH *18 minutes ago*

@AXEMANCOMETH: lol "God has a plan for all of us"
BLACKSHEEP34 *17 minutes ago*

@BLACKSHEEP34: Why don't you just keep your opinion to yourself? Religion gives people comfort in times of grief and loss... What's wrong with that?
TOMMYTELLER88 *15 minutes ago*

@TOMMYTELLER88: religion is a joke and a con, to get stupid people to stay docile and not take ownership of their lives. It always has been and always will be.
BLACKSHEEP34 *14 minutes ago*

This is so so so so very SAD. My heart goes out to these poor people.
BITTYCITY7 *13 minutes ago*

You think this is funny?

Melissa Nevis joined Facebook. *25 minutes ago*

Melissa Nevis changed her profile picture. *24 minutes ago*

Melissa Nevis added **swimming really hard for a long time** and **hogging all of the media's attention** to her **Interests**. *22 minutes ago*

Melissa Nevis added **don't go chasing waterfalls by t.l.c.** to her **Favorite Music**. *21 minutes ago*

Melissa Nevis wrote on her own wall: Hi everybody! *20 minutes ago*

Melissa Nevis is now friends with Gavin Reilly and Vicky Michael. *20 minutes ago*

Melissa Nevis is now friends with Fran Carlson and Bob Humphrey. *19 minutes ago*

Melissa Nevis is now friends with Dee Cramer, Molly Harper, and Gina Dewitt. *18 minutes ago*

Molly Harper wrote on Melissa Nevis's wall: You think this is funny? I only friended you so that I could write on your wall and tell you that you are disgusting. *18 minutes ago.*

Xandra Michael, Scott Pinkerton, and 3 other people like Molly Harper's comment. *17 minutes ago*

Melissa Nevis is now friends with Craig Kildare, Sasha Monroe, Willie McBride, and Jeff McIntosh. *16 minutes ago*

Melissa Nevis commented on her picture: Quite a ride! *15 minutes ago*

Craig Kildare wrote on Melissa Nevis's wall: Take everything else away, the idea that a six-year-old would put together this fb profile is ridiculous. Beyond that, everything else is in such bad taste that it hardly merits comment. *14 minutes ago*

Melissa Nevis joined the Facebook group **One Million Prayers for Melissa Nevis**. *13 minutes ago*

Melissa Nevis wrote on the wall for the Facebook group **One Million Prayers for Melissa Nevis**: Thanks for all the support you guys! You guys rock!!!! Smooches!!!! *12 minutes ago*

Melissa Nevis's profile has been reported to Facebook for the reason: Fraudulent Account. *11 minutes ago*

Melissa Nevis's profile has has been deleted by the Administrator. *10 minutes ago*

Your search for melissa nevis

Your search for *melissa nevis* produced 943 results

Title: **Looking for Melissa**
Uploaded by: FrankNevis *7 days ago*
Duration: 2:35
45,032 views / 3 likes / 0 dislikes

Tags: *gill falls, gill falls girl, melissa nevis, waterfall, search and rescue*

Description: Looking for Melissa in the woods below the falls... Please keep us all in your prayers

See more results like this

Title: **Dinner at home**

Uploaded by: FrankNevis *6 days ago*

Duration: 1:59

345 views / 0 likes / 0 dislikes

Tags: *gill falls, gill falls girl, melissa nevis, waterfall, search and rescue*

Description: Dinner at home, waiting on news of Melissa

See more results like this

Title: **Going through the garage**

Uploaded by: FrankNevis *7 days ago*

Duration: 3:15

481 views / 2 likes / 5 dislikes

Tags: *gill falls, gill falls girl, melissa nevis, waterfall, search and rescue*

Description: Going through the garage where the boat was anchored, trying to figure out what happened

See more results like this

"We're not giving up hope."

...Thank you Gail. I'm here with Frank and Victoria Nevis and their children Sandra, Billy, June, and Tommy. Frank and Victoria, thank you for being here with us today.

Thank you, Bill. We appreciate everyone's concern and... compassion.

Certainly, of course. If you would, tell us a little bit about your daughter Melissa. I know that everyone out there, they watch the news and they read the papers and they see this just adorable little girl, and they have a name and a face but they don't know Melissa the way that... the way that her family does. Victoria?

Yes Melissa is our youngest she's everyone's little... everyone's little sister. Right guys? And she's just... she's just the sweetest, most caring little soul. She's just like a... like a ray of sunshine when she comes into the room.

I know that this is difficult and I appreciate you talking with us today. I know that there are a lot of people out there who have heard the story and who want to help, want to do what they can to help you find your daughter and to basically rebuild your lives after this terrible, terrible tragedy.

Yes that's absolutely true people have been just wonderful to us. Just, you cannot believe how wonderful people can be at a time like this.

That's right we are just so, so very grateful to all of the wonderful people out there who have taken the time out of their lives to help us. We just feel so very blessed.

Thank you Victoria and thank you Frank. I know you've got a lot of work to do and I know you're all still down at the river every day with the search crews. I wonder if you would comment before we let you go here if you wouldn't mind letting our viewers know what the plan is now from down on the ground, in the search efforts, what's going on there.

Well we, uh... we're walking the river and they have divers in searching... uh, we're just, you know, we're praying for a miracle, praying that somehow... You know you never know with these things. Nobody was there, nobody saw what happened after the, uh, after the boat went over so we're just keeping our hearts open and we're not... We're not giving up hope.

Thank you Frank and thank you Victoria and thank you kids for being here with us. From Gill Falls, Missouri, I'm Bill Conrad. Back to you, Gail.

Nevis Family: "We're not giving up hope."

www.NNC.com/Frank_Nevis_not_giving_up.html
3 hours ago

In an exclusive interview with World News Network reporter Bill Conrad, Frank Nevis stated that he and his family were continuing in their search for their daughter Melissa, who has been missing since last Saturday when the boat she was riding in was carried over the Gill Falls Waterfall by the flood-swollen river.

"We're not giving up hope," said Frank Nevis, in reply to questions regarding the state of the search. He added, however, that he and his family were "praying for a miracle."

Melissa Nevis has been missing since last Saturday. The vessel she was riding in, an experimental watercraft designed by her father, was recovered from the river late Monday night, though Melissa's body was not found on-board.

Johnny Deider posted a link on the wall for the group **One Million Prayers for Melissa Nevis:** *www.NNC.com/ Frank_Nevis_not_giving_up.html 5 minutes ago*

Johnny Deider posted a link on the wall for the group **One Million Prayers for Melissa Nevis:** *www.YouTube .com/ user/WNN/Franknevisinterview?blend=1&ob=5#p/ f/2/8c6tcrwwTto 5 minutes ago 4 likes 0 dislikes*

Johnny Deider commented on his post: Vid of an interview with Frank and the fam... *4 minutes ago*

Jen Mathis commented on Johnny Deider's post: Thanks for posting... These people have been through so much and are still so strong... an inspiration *3 minutes ago*

Dotty Miller wrote on the wall for the group **One Million Prayers for Melissa Nevis:** I may not have all of the answers, but I know someone who does. HE watches over us all, day and night. There is nothing HE can't do. HE gave sight to the blind, made the lame walk, and raised the dead. REPOST IF YOU BELIEVE IN MIRACLES!!!! *2 minutes ago*

Jen Mathis wrote on the wall for the group **One Million Prayers for Melissa Nevis:** I may not have all of the answers, but I know someone who does. HE watches over us all, day and night. There is nothing HE can't do. HE gave sight to the blind, made the lame walk, and raised the dead. REPOST IF YOU BELIEVE IN MIRACLES!!!! *1 minute ago*

David Green wrote on the wall for the group **One Million Prayers for Melissa Nevis:** I may not have all of the answers, but I know someone who does. HE watches over us all, day and night. There is nothing HE can't do. HE gave sight to the blind, made the lame walk, and raised the dead. REPOST IF YOU BELIEVE IN MIRA-CLES!!!! *1 minute ago*

Dotty Long wrote on the wall for the group **One Million Prayers for Melissa Nevis:** I may not have all of the answers, but I know someone who does. HE watches over us all, day and night. There is nothing HE can't do. HE gave sight to the blind, made the lame walk, and raised the dead. REPOST IF YOU BELIEVE IN MIRACLES!!!! *1 minute ago*

The guidelines outlined in the literature

...And we're speaking with Anne Giardano, author of the book *Search and Destroy: How the Politics and Policies of Search and Rescue Agencies Do More Harm Than Good* and Phil Armstrong, head of the National Search and Rescue Association. Thank you both for being with us.

Thank you. Thank you for having me.

Thank you, Charlie.

Anne you say in your book that the culture of litigation that has sprung up around rescue personnel, be they paramedics or doctors or firefighters, in the last forty years has seriously hampered their ability to effectively fulfill their stated duties. Do you feel that this is the case in this most recent incident, with, uh, with what happened in Gill Falls? The situation with the little girl going over the waterfall?

Absolutely Charlie you know I spoke earlier with Frank Nevis that's the girl, her name is Melissa, that's her father I spoke earlier with Mr. Nevis and he told me that he told the rescue workers on the scene that his daughter was being carried downriver in the seconds after it happened, and that even though he made clear to them the necessity, the, uh, the limited time that they had rescue workers still had to go speak with their superiors, had to get the all clear before proceeding with a rescue.

And no rescue was attempted, I should say no rescue was attempted by rescue personnel I wonder if Phil Armstrong if you could comment on that decision.

Well of course I wasn't on the ground during that specific situation but it is always... It always falls to the director to make the call at the time... I've spoken with Bill Brixley, with, uh, Fire Chief Bill Brixley and I've reviewed the facts of this situation and in my opinion and by the guidelines outlined in the literature Bill made the right call... There were many other people in need of aid, time was running out, the information they had told them that the situation was only going to get worse...

...Charlie, if I could...

...was, um, only going to get worse...

Charlie, this is exactly what I'm talking about... The guidelines outlined in the literature said that rescuers shouldn't go try to save Melissa Nevis I mean, what kind of answer is that? What kind of answer is that to Melissa's mother and father?

...Anne thank you for that let's give Phil a chance to finish... Phil?

...I was just going to say that the bottom line, the number one rule of all Search and Rescue is that you never put yourself in a situation where you yourself might have to be rescued... I mean if you've got twenty guys trying to evacuate a hundred people and suddenly you take a big stupid risk, now you've got two or five or however many guys trying to save you... We are there we are on the scene to help, and we can't be of help if we're the ones who need help. People...

...Thank you Phil oh I'm sorry go ahead.

... Oh I was just going to say people have this expectation that because we're on the scene in this capacity, that if we don't save somebody that we've somehow failed... A lot of guys... this is a major issue within the S and R community as well guys walk around with tremendous guilt because they weren't able to save this guy or that guy but the fact of the matter is when we get called in it's because things have gone really, really bad, you understand? And not everybody can be saved. And to try to save some people in some situations is just going to get more guys killed.

...Thank you Phil I wonder if...

So you're telling me, excuse me Charlie, you're telling me that Melissa Nevis, that in this situation one of those rescuers couldn't have taken a boat out and pulled Melissa Nevis's boat back to safety, you're telling me the five minutes that would have taken, that they shouldn't have done that?

... Again I was not there, it's not fair for me to speculate one way or the other, but I do know that Bill Brixley made the call that to go out into the open river in a boat would have put his man at undue risk and I stand behind that call. Bill Brixley is a competent and decorated public servant and I and the National S and R Association stand behind him and his decision.

So, you think that...

I'm terribly sorry Anne I have to cut you off there just for a moment we will be back in just one minute with more from Anne Giardano, author of the book *Search and Destroy*, and Phil Armstrong, head of the National Search and Rescue Association. Back in one minute.

Customer Reviews for the title: **Search and Destroy: How the Politics and Policies of Search and Rescue Agencies Do More Harm Than Good** by Anne Giardano

"A Broken System" by Judy Neil (Sarasota, Fl)
Star Rating: 4/5
30 of 35 people found this review helpful.

I happened across a radio interview with Anne Giardano, and decided to pick up her book **Search and Destroy: How the Politics and Policies of Search and Rescue Agencies do more Harm than Good**. Ms. Giardano writes with a kind of terse, no-nonsense tone, and by the end of the first chapter I was sitting up in my chair and paying attention.

She begins the book with a brief history of what are now, as she calls them, the "Big Four": the Police, Fire & Emergency, the National Guard, and the various other Search and Rescue Agencies under the oversight of the National Government. In the next section, she outlines the key lawsuits that have come to define a lot of the policies for these agencies. She then chronicles the way in which recent political decisions have affected them.

Coming into this book I knew very little about Search and Rescue and had always assumed, I guess kind of optimistically, that if something bad ever happened to me or to someone I loved, that someone would come in and save the day. Reading through the various accounts of rescues aborted (the author spends a great deal of time tracing policy decisions through to their on-the-scene ramifications, down to the grisly details, so squeamish readers be warned) sent a shiver down my spine.

At times this book reads more like a manifesto than journalism, and I found myself wondering if there wasn't more that the author was leaving out. Still, what was included was eye-opening. I would definitely recommend.

Help other readers find the most helpful reviews.
Was this review helpful to you? Yes No

"search and destroy... this book" by Jim Fischer (Omaha, Ne)
Star Rating: 1/5
21 of 48 people found this review helpful

Reading this book is like taking driving advice from an 8-year-old. Ms. Giardano has never worked for any Search and Rescue agency. She was never so much as a crossing guard. I gave this book a 1 out of 5 stars, and it only got the one because you can't give 0.

I have been a firefighter for 22 years, and because of that somebody thought this book would be of interest to me. I hope next time they give me a gift they just kick me in the gut instead. Aside from implying that rescue workers (people who risk their necks for other people who are often in harm's way because of their own stupidity) are a bunch of wimps hiding behind policy, this book disregards THOUSANDS AND THOUSANDS of successful rescues to focus on a few moments when rescuers couldn't help. To Ms. Giardano I have to say: these men live every day with the fact that there are people that they couldn't help. That's what they see when they close their eyes at night. What do you see? A big pile of money and the desk where you sit and don't risk anything for anybody.

Help other readers find the most helpful reviews.

So I said to myself, enough is enough

We are interrupting our regularly scheduled broadcast to bring you this breaking story. Just moments ago it was confirmed that Melissa Nevis, the six-year-old resident of Gill Falls, Missouri, who nine days ago was reportedly carried over the Gill Falls Waterfall by the flood-swollen river, and who rescue crews have been searching tirelessly for since her subsequent disappearance, has been found alive. We go live to Gene Varijou, on the scene.

Thank you Bill I'm here in Headon, Missouri, a small rural community located a little more than one hundred miles east of Gill Falls, and I am standing in front of the home of Mrs. Barbara Lagrange, Victoria Nevis's mother and maternal grandmother to Melissa Nevis. Now thirty minutes ago Mrs. Lagrange called local police to tell them that in fact Melissa Nevis had been staying with her for the past ten days. Earlier she met briefly with members of the press, and had this to say:

... Finally I said to myself, enough is enough. People have been sending them money they've been sending checks they've been going down personally to help and it's not right. I'm not going to be part of it anymore.

So Gene what we're understanding at this point is that Melissa Nevis's disappearance, that the boat going over the falls, was all some sort of... elaborate... uh, prank perpetuated by the girl's parents? Are we understanding you correctly?

That's exactly right Bill that is how the situation appears here in Headon.

Have you been able to get a sense or is there any indi-cation as to what the reason was behind this? I mean, ob-viously this was planned out, uh, to some extent, this was a premeditated, um, uh... sort of situation.

Um, Bill at this point we have been unable to speak with either Mrs. Lagrange or Melissa's parents... We have been told that Mrs. Lagrange is being questioned by po-lice but again we have been unable to speak with Mrs. Lagrange and police have refused to make any statement until they have concluded their investigation into what actually occurred.

But again, for all intents and purposes, at this point it appears that this was some sort of elaborate hoax, this was all a, uh, a charade of sorts perpetuated by Melissa's par-ents by Frank and Victoria Nevis.

That is certainly the situation as it seems here in Hea-don.

Well thank you Gene now we will bring you more on this breaking story as it develops, and for now we will return you to your regularly scheduled, uh, programming.

Bo Todd posted a link...

Bo Todd posted a link on the wall for the group **One Million Prayers for Melissa Nevis**: http://www.you tube.com/user/flygirl/barbaralagrangeuncutinterview/watc h?v=I9tWZB7OUSU&feature=related *3 minutes ago 4 likes 0 dislikes*

Vick Billings posted a link on the wall for the group **One Million Prayers for Melissa Nevis**: http://www.youtube.com/user/flygirl/barbaralagrangeuncu

tinterview/watch?v=I9tWZB7OUSU&feature=related *3 minutes ago*

Bob Tucker posted a link on the wall for the group **One Million Prayers for Melissa Nevis**: http://www.you tube.com/user/flygirl/barbaralagrangeuncutinterview/watc h?v=I9tWZB7OUSU&feature=related *2 minutes ago*

Comments:

Dave Michaelson wrote: Fanfrickingtastic

Nick Parker posted a link on the wall for the group **One Million Prayers for Melissa Nevis**: http://www.you tube.com/user/flygirl/Barbara_Lagrange_uncut_interview/ watch?v=I9tWZB7OUSU&feature=related

---

Your search for melissa nevis found

Your search for *melissa nevis found* produced 1,200 results

Title: **Barbara Lagrange uncut interview**
Uploaded by: FlyGirl *1 hour ago*
Duration: 1:03
45,211 views / 2,190 likes / 6 dislikes
Description: the uncut interview with Barbara La-grange in which she reveals that Melissa Nevis has been safe and sound the entire time rescue crews were looking for her... MELISSA NEVIS FOUND INTERVIEW BAR-BARA LAGRANGE
See more results like this

Title: **Barbara Lagrange full interview**
Uploaded by: LegalizeIt420 *1 hour ago*
Duration: 1:03

25,342 views / 2,000 likes / 0 dislikes
Description: MELISSA NEVIS FOUND barbara lagrange frank nevis
See more results like this

Title: **Barbara Lagrange interview FULL**
Uploaded by: GUNSOFBRIXTON *1 hour ago*
Duration: 1:03
34,021 views / 210 likes / 0 dislikes
Description: melissa nevis has been found turns out she was hanging out with her grandma the entire time THE NEVISES ARE BAD PEOPLE
See more results like this

Title: **INTERVIEW: Barbara Lagrange**
Uploaded by: RasBabo1 *35 minutes ago*
Duration: 1:03
12,239 views / 149 likes / 0 dislikes
Description: *no description available*
See more results like this

Title: **Melissa Nevis has been found!!!!!**
Uploaded by: ViceRoy134 *4 days ago*
Duration: 4:13
162,342 views / 900 likes / 1,305 dislikes
Description: During the flooding in the town of Gill Falls, MO. six-year-old Melissa Nevis was carried away by the rising river. Now the boat she was in has been found...
See more results like this

Title: **Melissa We Love You**
Uploaded by: FrankNevis *2 days ago*
Duration: 1:05

253,392 views / 451 likes / 5 dislikes

Description: A message to Melissa Nevis from your family

See more results like this

Title: **A Father's Plea: Help Me Find My Daughter**
Uploaded by: FrankNevis *7 days ago*
Duration: 0:45
2,590,234 views / 100,000 likes / 35 dislikes

Description: Cell phone video looking for my daughter thanx every1 for prayers and support GOD BLESS YOU

See more results like this

Barbara Lagrange Uncut Interview

Title: **Barbara Lagrange uncut interview**
Uploaded by: FlyGirl *2 hours ago*
Duration: 1:03
57,211 views / 3,291 likes / 8 dislikes

Description: the uncut interview with Barbara Lagrange in which she reveals that Melissa Nevis has been safe and sound the entire time rescue crews were looking for her... MELISSA NEVIS FOUND INTERVIEW BARBARA LAGRANGE

I'm not going to stand out here and answer a... answer a bunch of your questions I just came out to set the record straight... that... to tell everyone that my granddaughter, Melissa Nevis, is fine, she's with me, she didn't go over any waterfall... I took her to my home because my son-in-law and my daughter asked me they said there's going to be flooding, we're worried about Melissa and the kids, so I said all right, I came and picked her up drove right in the direction they told me not to go all the police and everybody said not to go I picked her up from their house and the next thing I know I see on the news they're saying she's gone over a waterfall in this boat... I called my daughter and I couldn't get a hold of her and then when I finally could she said just don't say anything mama, just for a day or two, please just keep Melissa there it's very important so I said Vicki, you're my daughter and I love you, and I'll do it because you ask me to... But things have gotten so crazy... I'm watching the news and they're talking about dragging the river and interviews and people writing articles finally I said to myself, enough is enough... people have been sending them money they've been sending checks they've been coming down personally to help and it's not right... I'm not going to be part of it anymore. That's all I have to say. My granddaughter is fine. Now please, everybody, just leave us alone.

An unexpected development

... Well an unexpected development tonight in the on-going story of Melissa Nevis, the so-called "Gill Falls Girl," who authorities had believed was carried over the Gill Falls Waterfall during the flooding in Gill Falls, Missouri some ten days ago. In a video interview with several members of the press Mrs. Barbara Lagrange, Melissa's maternal grandmother, revealed that in fact Melissa had been with her the entire time. In a video that quickly went viral on the internet Mrs. Lagrange explains that she picked Melissa up from the Nevis's home some time before the evacuation of Gill Falls began. When she saw on the news that search crews were out looking for Melissa she called her daughter, who asked her to keep the family's secret. She says that she was willing to do so out of love for her daughter, but that after seeing the sensation it was causing, decided that it had gone far enough.

... I'm watching the news and they're talking about dragging the river and interviews and people writing articles finally I said to myself, enough is enough... people have been sending them money they've been sending checks they've been coming down personally to help and it's not right... I'm not going to be part of it anymore...

Obviously that was Barbara Lagrange, in her comments from earlier today. No word as of yet from Melissa's parents, although we have learned that police are questioning Frank and Victoria Nevis to try to determine just what exactly, uh, determine what exactly was, uh, going on.

Shocking news tonight

Well shocking news tonight out of Headon, Missouri, where Mrs. Barbara Lagrange has revealed that Melissa Nevis, the six-year-old girl authorities believed was carried over the Gill Falls Waterfall during the recent flooding, was in fact with her the entire time. Mrs. Lagrange is the mother of Victoria Nevis and, according to a statement she gave earlier today, was asked by her daughter to pick Melissa up from their home some time before the evacuation, and then to keep Melissa's location a secret during the subsequent search. No word yet from either Frank or

Victoria Nevis, but we are told that they are currently being questioned by police.

Gill Falls Girl Safe, Parents in Hot Water

by Dean Richardson, Guest Contributor

Gill Falls, MO - Melissa Nevis is finally able to go home, but her parents may not be there to welcome her.

Nine days after the vessel in which she was allegedly riding was carried over the Gill Falls Waterfall - sparking a massive search operation and an explosion of media coverage - it was revealed by Barbara Lagrange, Melissa's maternal grandmother, that Melissa was safe and sound and staying with her the entire time.

The relief felt by the millions who have been following this story (a Facebook group called **One Million Prayers for Melissa Nevis**, for example, had 1,341,987 members at the time of Mrs. LaGrange's announcement) was quickly replaced by outrage at Frank and Victoria Nevis, Melissa's parents, who Mrs. Lagrange named as responsible for the fraud.

"I called [Victoria] and she said just don't say anything mama," said Mrs. Lagrange, explaining that she was unaware of their plans when she picked Melissa up from their home.

As for Victoria and Frank, there is no word from them yet as to what they were trying to accomplish with their stunt, though many point to the fame and economic aid they have received as the likely cause. Whatever the gains, however, it may be a long time before they are in any position to enjoy it: at the time of this writing they are still being held for questioning by police.

Dean Richardson is a frequent contributor to the Herald-Sentinel. This article is available online at www.Herald Sentinel.com. Contact Dean Richardson by email at Dean Richardson@heraldsentinel.com.

www.NNN.com/Gill_Falls_Girl_Safe_Parents_in_Hot_ Water.html

Gill Falls, MO - Melissa Nevis is finally able to go home, but her parents may not be there to welcome her.

Nine days after the vessel in which she was allegedly riding was carried over the Gill Falls Waterfall - sparking a massive search operation and an explosion of media coverage - it was revealed by Barbara Lagrange, Melissa's maternal grandmother, that Melissa was safe and sound and staying with her the entire time.

The relief felt by the millions who have been following this story (a Facebook group called One Million Prayers for Melissa Nevis, for example, had 1,341,987 members at the time of Mrs. LaGrange's announcement) was quickly replaced by outrage at Frank and Victoria Nevis, Melissa's parents, who Mrs. Lagrange named as responsible for the fraud.

"I called [Victoria] and she said just don't say anything mama," said Mrs. Lagrange, explaining that she was unaware of their plans when she picked Melissa up from their home.

As for Victoria and Frank, there is no word from them yet as to what they were trying to accomplish with their stunt, though many point to the fame and economic aid they have received as the likely cause. Whatever the gains, however, it may be a long time before they arc in any position to enjoy it: at the time of this writing they are still being held for questioning by police.

by Dean Richardson
Source*: www.HeraldSentinel.com/Gill_Falls_Girl_Safe_P arents_in_Hot_Water.html*

www.LiveNewsSource.com/Gill_Falls_Girl_Safe_Parent s_in_Hot_Water.html

Gill Falls, MO - Melissa Nevis is finally able to go home, but her parents may not be there to welcome her.

Nine days after the vessel in which she was allegedly riding was carried over the Gill Falls Waterfall - sparking a massive search operation and an explosion of media coverage - it was revealed by Barbara Lagrange, Melissa's maternal grandmother, that Melissa was safe and sound and staying with her the entire time.

The relief felt by the millions who have been following this story (a Facebook group called One Million Prayers for Melissa Nevis, for example, had 1,341,987 members at the time of Mrs. LaGrange's announcement) was quickly replaced by outrage at Frank and Victoria Nevis, Melissa's parents, who Mrs. Lagrange named as responsible for the fraud.

"I called [Victoria] and she said just don't say anything mama," said Mrs. Lagrange, explaining that she was unaware of their plans when she picked Melissa up from their home.

As for Victoria and Frank, there is no word from them yet as to what they were trying to accomplish with their stunt, though many point to the fame and economic aid they have received as the likely cause. Whatever the gains, however, it may be a long time before they are in any position to enjoy it: at the time of this writing they are still being held for questioning by police.

by Dean Richardson
Source*: www.HeraldSentinel.com/Gill_Falls_Girl_Safe_P arents_in_Hot_Water.html*

www.WorldNewsCorp.com/Gill_Falls_Girl_Safe_Parent s_in_Hot_Water.html

Gill Falls, MO - Melissa Nevis is finally able to go home, but her parents may not be there to welcome her.

Nine days after the vessel in which she was allegedly riding was carried over the Gill Falls Waterfall - sparking a massive search operation and an explosion of media coverage - it was revealed by Barbara Lagrange, Melissa's maternal grandmother, that Melissa was safe and sound and staying with her the entire time.

The relief felt by the millions who have been following this story (a Facebook group called One Million Prayers for Melissa Nevis, for example, had 1,341,987 members at the time of Mrs. LaGrange's announcement) was quickly replaced by outrage at Frank and Victoria Nevis, Melissa's parents, who Mrs. Lagrange named as responsible for the fraud.

"I called [Victoria] and she said just don't say anything mama," said Mrs. Lagrange, explaining that she was unaware of their plans when she picked Melissa up from their home.

As for Victoria and Frank, there is no word from them yet as to what they were trying to accomplish with their stunt, though many point to the fame and economic aid they have received as the likely cause. Whatever the gains, however, it may be a long time before they are in any position to enjoy it: at the time of this writing they are still being held for questioning by police.

by Dean Richardson
Source*: www.HeraldSentinel.com/Gill_Falls_Girl_Safe_P arents_in_Hot_Water.html*

Gone but not forgotten

@MyNews16
Breaking news on the Melissa Nevis story see more at www.mynews16.com *26 minute ago*

@BravoDelta9er
GILL FALLS GIRL WAS A HOAX?!?!?. *25 minute ago*

@RightSaidFred
Damn... Just when my heart had learned to trust again... I should have learned after bubble boy!!!! I should have learned!!! *22 minutes ago*

@WorldWideNewsNetwork
Breaking news in Melissa Nevis story live streaming at www.WWNN.com *21 minute ago*

@DarcyLovesParsley
   @RightSaidFred: LOL *21 minutes ago*

@MyNetisBigger
   I think most people underestimate how effective it
   can be, pretending your child is at risk to draw
   attention to yourself. Frank and Victoria, you have
   opened my eyes, you loathsome pieces of shit *21
   minutes ago*

@RicoEndive
   @MyNetisBigger: word brother. *20 minutes ago*

@BobN4apples
   RIP Gill Falls Girl... another media sensation gone
   but not forgotten *20 minutes ago*

@WorldWideNewsNetwork
   Breaking news in Melissa Nevis story live streaming at www.WWNN.com *19 minute ago*

@MyNews16
   Breaking news on the Melissa Nevis story see
   more at www.mynews16.com *18 minute ago*

@SpilledMilk
   What? You're telling me the news media charged
   ahead without knowing what was really going on,
   and then blew a situation way out of proportion?
   No, not in the USA! *17 minute ago*

@JungleLuv

FRANK AND VICTORIA NEVIS R DISGUST-
ING MONSTERS WHO'S CHILDREN NEED
TO BE TAKEN AWAY FOR THERE OWN
SAFETY *16 minutes ago*

@BoPeep23
This gill falls girl story is so sad on every level...
the desire to be famous makes people absolutely
crazy... it's sick *15 minutes ago*

@DropItLikeItsHAWT
I liked her better when she was missing... it was
like a scavenger hunt the whole country was playing. find the gill falls girl! *14 minutes ago*

@FossilizedRemains
I was in the field for the past two weeks, and am
hearing about the gill falls girl for the first time
today... i laughed so hard that coke came out my
nose *13 minutes ago*

@Magneto09
@FossilizedRemains: coke is supposed to go in
your nose, not out of it *12 minutes ago*

@LoolooVoodoo
Goodonya barbara lagrange... way to be a good
person... NINE DAYS AFTER IT WOULD HAVE
BEEN HELPFUL *11 minutes ago*

Ginny Fordham left the group **One Million Prayer for Melissa Nevis.** *13 minutes ago*

Drake Smith left the group **One Million Prayers for Melissa Nevis.** *13 minutes ago*

Carrie Anne left the group **One Million Prayers for Melissa Nevis.** *12 minutes ago*

Kiki Lewis left the group **One Million Prayers for Melissa Nevis.** *12 minutes ago*

Alex Laramie wrote on the wall for the group **One Million Prayers for Melissa Nevis:** So long, Gill Falls Girl. It was good while it lasted. *11 minutes ago 6 likes 0 dislikes*

Alex Laramie left the group **One Million Prayers for Melissa Nevis.** *11 minutes ago*

Vince Drake, Maggie Peters, Jane Fellis, and 3 other people left the group **One Million Prayers for Melissa Nevis.** *10 minutes ago*

Jenny Miller wrote on the wall for the group **One Million Prayers for Melissa Nevis:** ok guys i'm deleting this page... you should all still feel good about being members... everybody was tricked by some dishonest people, but showing compassion for a stranger is what makes the world a better place... God bless. *9 minutes ago*

The group **One Million Prayers for Melissa Nevis** has been deleted by the Administrator. *8 minutes ago*

Mike Fowler created the group **One Million People Who Think Frank Nevis is a Lying Douchebag.** *30 minutes ago*

Mike Fowler wrote on the wall for the group **One Million People Who Think Frank Nevis is a Lying Douchebag:** hello everyone "like" this page if you think frank and victoria nevis are lying douchebags whose kids should be taken away from them!! Thanx!!! *29 minutes ago*

Leone Randall joined the group **One Million People Who Think Frank Nevis is a Lying Douchebag.** *28 minutes ago*

Diedrich Vastich joined the group **One Million People Who Think Frank Nevis is a Lying Douchebag.** *27 minutes ago*

Molly Pedderton joined the group **One Million People Who Think Frank Nevis is a Lying Douchebag.** *27 minutes ago*

Scott Angeline joined the group **One Million People Who Think Frank Nevis is a Lying Douchebag.** *26 minutes ago*

Peter Miller joined the group **One Million People Who Think Frank Nevis is a Lying Douchebag.** *26 minutes ago*

Facebook wrote on the wall for the group **One Million People Who Think Frank Nevis is a Lying Douchebag:** It has been brought to Facebook's attention that this group may violate the Terms of Use. If you believe this was done in error, please contact us using the form below. *25 minutes ago*

Billy Dickinson joined the group **One Million People Who Think Frank Nevis is a Lying Douchebag.** *25 minutes ago*

Vicky Carmichael joined the group **One Million People Who Think Frank Nevis is a Lying Douchebag.** *24 minutes ago*

Kyle Lynch joined the group **One Million People Who Think Frank Nevis is a Lying Douchebag.** *24 minutes ago*

Drew Bower joined the group **One Million People Who Think Frank Nevis is a Lying Douchebag.** *23 minutes ago*

Facebook wrote on the wall for the group **One Million People Who Think Frank Nevis is a Lying Douchebag:** This group has been found to be in violation of the Terms of Use, and will be deleted. *22 minutes ago*

The group **One Million People Who Think Frank Nevis is a Lying Douchebag** has been deleted by Facebook. *21 minutes ago*

There's No Business Like Show Business - Nevis Style

www.MediaWatch.bloghost.com
We're watching them watching us watching them

Title: There's No Business Like Show Business - Nevis Style

Tags: Gill Falls Girl, Frank Nevis, Victoria Nevis, Hoax, Prank, Media Stunt, Melissa Nevis

By: Donny Tupper

I have put off commenting on the "Gill Falls Girl" situation for the sole reason that I consider it in bad taste to write about any ongoing tragedy in which one or more of those people affected might stumble across what I had written. I consider it in especially poor taste to do so in any situation involving the death (or the possible death) of a child. However, in this instance, it has become clear that the perpetuating parties are untroubled by any such questions of taste, and so I will withhold my commentary no longer.

Let's go back a few days - twelve days, to be exact - to the moment when the Gill River was just beginning to crest its banks and the order to evacuate had only just been issued. Frank and Victoria Nevis called Victoria's mother, Mrs. Barbara Lagrange, and asked that she drive in from her home in Headon one hundred miles east of Gill Falls (and far from any threat of flooding) to pick up their youngest daughter, Melissa. Being a loving mother and a devoted grandmother, and being concerned for the welfare of her relatives, she readily agreed and complied. It was not until some hours later, as she scanned the news for word on the flooding in Gill Falls, that she discovered that everyone else in the country believed Melissa was being carried over the Gill Falls Waterfall in an experimental watercraft designed by her [Barbara's] son-in-law.

Barbara Lagrange spent the following nine days in a state of near-constant psychic torment, unsure whether to comply with her daughter's further request - that she keep Melissa's safety and presence a secret - or go to the authorities with that information. Each time she turned on the television she hoped that there would be no mention of the "Gill Falls Girl" - that the story would slip from the spotlight and that Melissa could be quietly returned home. Each time she turned on the television, however, she was instead confronted by newscasters talking about her granddaughter, and interviews with her daughter and son-in-law, adding fuel to the fire. She didn't understand what was going on, or why. Why would anyone make it seem like their child had been carried away by the flood? Who would do such a thing? The obvious truth - that Frank and Victoria were cooly playing the news media (and through them, the entire nation) for their own personal gain - did not occur to her: she could not believe that her own daughter would be so callous, so unethical, so calculating and inhuman.

Love often blinds us to those truths we would rather not know about the ones we love, and often there is no unpleasant truth too big for that blindness to obscure it: it is only later, in hindsight, that we wonder how we went along without acknowledging or correcting some unendurable circumstance. The families of addicts are no stranger to this phenomenon: love and the desire not to know, on the part of family and friends, have allowed many addicts to maintain their addictions long after they have lost the ability to artfully mask its effects. The drug of choice for Frank and Victoria Nevis - the drug for which they lied to the entire country - was the euphoric rush of Fame.

Now let's go back ten years. Melissa Nevis hasn't been born - neither, in fact, have June or Tommy, Frank and Victoria's 7- and 8-year-old. With only two children to support Frank is able to make ends meet working part-time and still pursue his true passion: inventing. In February of 2001 and May of 2003 the U.S. Government issued patents to Frank Nevis. The inventions for which he received these patents - an oscillating blender and an accordion-style closet organizer - never brought Frank the attention or success he hoped they would, and in 2003 -

with newborn Tommy now straining the family's finances - Frank is forced to curtail his efforts and get a full-time job. (He never fully abandoned his first love, however, and filed a handful of further patents in the following years, though these were rejected as "not notably improved from the original design," a.k.a not original enough - to merit approval.)

It is during this period that Frank begins a second project: as he no longer has much time to tinker in the family's garage, he finds his creative outlet by pitching a reality show to various television networks. According to the transcript of the original pilot (Frank did eventually get someone to put up the money to make a pilot, although the show was obviously never picked up) the format was a fairly run-of-the-mill family-based reality show, with the added thread of Frank's inventions: each week Frank would come up with and attempt to manufacture an invention, while the various family dramas played out in the periphery. (One member of the test audience to which the pilot was shown said that Frank's "willingness to ignore his family for the sake of a retractable shoe rack [the invention in that episode] was too disturbing to be enjoyable viewing.")

With the failure of the pilot and now a fifth child to feed Frank has no choice but to forgo his dream of becoming a successful inventor / television personality almost entirely. He takes a second, part-time job, working nights stocking shelves at the local grocery store in Gill Falls. He is depressed by the failure of his various projects but he is also embittered by the experience, and feels that his efforts have been unappreciated by society in general. He watches other reality television shows, thinking that it should be him and his family on the television, should be him and his family making endorsement deals and moving into better neighborhoods. He feels marginalized and desperate, and this - combined with the feeling that he is being backed into a financial corner - sets the stage for what happened when the river rose above its banks and the order was given to evacuate.

Try, for a moment, to see society as a game in which advancement is earned through clever PR stunts, gimmicky attention grabs, and blatant and viral self-promotion. Try to see it as a kind of omnipotent banker, dispensing life-sustaining money with absolute autonomous authority and with executives and patent clerks as its minions. Try to see it, in effect, as Frank Nevis sees it, and you start to understand how he could do what he did: how he could crassly fabricate the death of his youngest child, lie to and manipulate an entire population, compel family members to lie in public, all in a perverse ploy for fortune and fame.

Posted by Donny Tupper 25 hours ago

Comments:

an interesting look at the whole gill falls girl situation... its so sad that ppl in the country seem to be willing to do any and everything just to be famous
posted by Anonymous *19 hours ago*

This would be really interesting if the author had any basis for half of what he says... is he a clinical psychologist, a close personal friend of the Nevis family? On what grounds does he make statements like "He is depressed by the failure of his various projects but he is also embittered by the experience"? Is this just postulation, or is there some source for this assessment?

This blog is a prime example of the dangers of death of the news media and the democratization of print.
posted by Franklin Summers *14 hours ago*

@FranklinSummers: everything I wrote about can be easily found with a quick google search for Frank Nevis... His patents are on file with the US Gov, his resume is on his LinkedIn page, a transcript of the pilot is available online, the ages of his children are public knowledge... The rest is obviously my own postulation as to what he might have been thinking or feeling at the time... then again, i never claimed this was pure "journalism"...
posted by Donny Tupper *13 hours ago*

I agree with Franklin move out of your mom's basement and take a journalism class...
posted by DixonMason *12 hours ago*

It makes me sad that people who don't have the chops to be actual journalists now have the excuse that newspapers are not hiring people... they can go on the web and blog and play out their little fantasy of being a journalist... posers
posted by YoMAMA1234 *11 hours ago*

"Love often blinds us to those truths we would rather not know about the ones we love, and often there is no unpleasant truth too big for that blindness to obscure it: it is only later, in hindsight, that we wonder how we went along without acknowledging or correcting some unendurable circumstance..." ... fucking *awesome* line man...
posted by JHawk78 *9 hours ago*

@JHawk78: Thanx man
posted by Donny Tupper *9 hours ago*

John Hawk wrote...

John Hawk posted a link to his wall: *www.Media Watch.bloghost.com/archive/Theres_No_Business_Like_S how_Business_Nevis_Style.html 8 hours ago*
John Hawk commented on his link: This blog does a really nice job of shedding light on Frank Nevis's background... anybody following the gill falls girl situation should definitely read *8 hours ago 5 comments 9 people like this*

Ulric Barabes commented on John Hawk's post: very interesting, thanx for sharing! *6 hours ago*

Gretta Brueger commented on John Hawk's post: there is NOTHING people won't do to get famous! What the hell is the world coming to?!?!? *6 hours ago*

Fred Mahoney commented on John Hawk's post: I gotta agree with the guy who said that this blog is what happens when anybody can write stuff that everybody else can read... even with the stuff he has researched, the guy takes some pretty serious liberties with the facts... *5 hours ago 2 people like this*

Erin Vargis commented on John Hawk's post: interesting stuff thanx for posting *4 hours ago*

Todd Pepper commented on John Hawk's post: hmmm.... *4 hours ago*

John Hawk wrote on his wall: "Love often blinds us to those truths we would rather not know about the ones we love, and often there is no unpleasant truth too big for that blindness to obscure it: it is only later, in hindsight, that we wonder how we went along without acknowledging or correcting some unendurable circumstance..." *3 hours ago 7 people like this*

Tonight: A Look Behind the Scenes

Tonight on Carlson Peters Live, a look behind the scenes at the Gill Falls Girl hoax. I'm Carlson Peters, and I'm joined tonight by Dr. Janet Boeing, author of the book *Know Thyself: An Owner's Manuel for the Modern Psyche*, Bill Brixley, Fire Chief of Gill Falls, Missouri, and Sarah Carter, the Nevis family's neighbor in Gill Falls. Good evening to you all, and good evening to everyone at home. Fire Chief Brixley I wonder if we could start with you... You've said in interviews that when you arrived at the scene to help the Nevis family evacuate you never saw Melissa Nevis, but that Frank Nevis immediately began telling you that she had likely gone to hide in the boat, which apparently she often did when she was frightened. Did that strike you as suspicious at the time, how forthcoming or how aggressive he was with that story?

Well, I believe I said in those interviews that I was not the first responder at the Nevis home, that two of my crew were there, and I got it from them that that is what he said.

Oh I see well I wonder if they mentioned that his behavior was at all suspicious?

Uh... they didn't but you have to understand that people in stressful situations like the one we were in that night don't act the way they might just, uh, just walking around everyday. So strange behavior is a little bit par for the course.

I see so they did not find it suspicious.

Not that they mentioned, no.

All right Sarah Carter you have lived next to the Nevis family for fourteen years, I wonder if you could give us an impression of what that was like, if there is anything you feel that people need to know about them that they might not be getting from the media.

I... No, I don't think so, I mean... They're just normal neighbors, you see them around and say hello... Uh, no I don't think there's anything in particular about them.

And Sarah we see that your hand is bandaged there... Is that from the rescue attempt?

Yes when we were trying to retrieve the boat from the river my hand got pinned between the railing and the rope we were using, and I fractured a couple of bones.

Oh dear well we hope that is healing satisfactorily tell us is there any resentment, you having suffered this injury for what turned out to be not a, uh, for what was essentially a fabrication?

Uh... Well... I mean, I still am proud of what I did what we all did on the bridge, we were going on the information at that time and... I don't think people realize just how devastated we all were when our plan didn't work, people on that bridge were just screaming and crying we thought we had basically let this little girl fall to her death, so I would have to say that, even under the circumstances, when we heard that she was safe, that Melissa Nevis was safe the first thing I felt was overwhelming relief.

I see. Dr. Boeing in your book you talk about how the American mentality has changed in the last, well since World War II... You make the statement that after World War II people began defining themselves and their expectations of themselves basically by making comparisons to their neighbors... uh, but you also say that now, that now we as a culture increasingly look to just a small handful of celebrities for that same comparison, I wonder if you would comment on that for any viewers who haven't read the book.

That's right Carlson in the years following the second World War what you saw was the explosion of the suburbs, it was boom time for the suburbs. Everyone could afford a home and so what you had was a lot of people who would otherwise be living in rural communities living almost right on top of each other, and the culture that occurred was very insular... You defined yourself largely in comparison with the limited context of your immediate environment.

You make the point that despite its limitations, that this mode of life was actually more conducive to happiness than some of its modern versions.

That's right when you have such a limited sphere it is much easier to add value to your context. In the fifties you saw all of these community organizations springing up all over the place. People were aware that the broader world was out there, but it was enough for them to have a place in their own community.

And you say that that has changed significantly.

Yes, somewhere along the line what happened was that it was no longer good enough to be somebody in your hometown, you had to be somebody on a national or a global scale... And a few things brought this about but most notably the change in the way we use technology, the way technology has made the world accessible, has made us so aware of the world beyond our own little sphere, and then I think another big part of it a part that people don't talk about very much is that the children of the boomers, the children born in the seventies and eighties were born during a trend in the child-rearing culture that said children need to be pushed, the idea was that children were this sort of blank slate and that if you started early enough your child could be a prodigy cello player or a concert pianist or a brilliant artist. So you have this younger generation that has been told, basically, you could always be more than you are, you could always be a better version of yourself, and that is just a recipe for unhappiness.

And we're going to come back to you Bill Brixley in just one second but Dr. Boeing just to sort of sum up the idea then is that fame becomes a, um, a much bigger, um, priority shall we say.

Exactly Carlson it's a matter of feeling good about what you contribute, what value you add to your surroundings, and the situation we face these days is that, one, because of the internet and international news our quote-unquote surrounds have become the entire country, if not the world, and, two, that the only people who add value on this kind of a scale are huge celebrities. So people see this, they say I was told I could be anything growing up, I could be rich or famous if I worked harder, or was better at my job, or whatever the case may be with them, and at the end of the day they can't feel good about what they've done because it didn't achieve this almost impossibly high mark.

Interesting stuff and we'll have more with Dr. Boeing in just a moment but now I want to go back to Fire Chief Bill Brixley, um, and ask you if you would to just tell us a little bit your feelings on this situation.

Uh, well... The situation... It's frustrating to think of the hours the crews wasted searching the river and, I mean, every time somebody goes out into the field in that sort of a situation there's some risk involved, now in hindsight it was obviously a good decision and at the time it was the right decision not to send the crews out to try to recover the craft at the time that it was first carried away by the floodwaters... Uh, if men had gone out to retrieve it you just... You never know what might have happened so my feelings might be a, uh, a little bit different but thankfully that wasn't the case.

Thank you Fire Chief Brixley and we'll have more with all of my guests after this short break, stay with us.

Tonight! Greg Morgan sits down with Barbara Lagrange

Tonight, Greg Morgan sits down with Barbara Lagrange for the exclusive interview America has been waiting for.

Greg Morgan: Why did they do it?

Barbara Lagrange: I think what they want... They want what everybody wants.

America has been waiting for answers. Tonight, no question is off limits.

Greg Morgan: Do you love your daughter?

Barbara Lagrange: I am upset with my daughter. I will always love my daughter.

Tonight at nine, the only place to watch is WNN. Check your local listings or go to WorldNewsNetwork. com to watch the video streaming online.

Bob Fuller posted on his own wall: OH MY GOD I DON'T CARE ABOUT MELISSA NEVIS!!!!! AM I ALONE IN THIS? *20 minutes ago 7 comments*

Kim Cooper commented on Bob Fuller's post: TO-TALLY *15 minutes ago*

Gill Kristopher commented on Bob Fuller's post: Couldn't agree with you more *12 minutes ago*

Hannah Brown commented on Bob Fuller's post: I think in a general way the whole thing is kind of interesting, but I have to admit I'm getting sick of hearing about it every time I turn on the damn tv... *10 minutes ago*

Frank Grove commented on Bob Fuller's post: "Fame: it's not your brain, it's just the flame, that burns your change to keep you insane." - David Bowie *7 minutes ago 1 person likes this*

Tom Eastman: They're going to end up with a reality TV show out of this (which, unfortunately, I think was the point) *4 minutes ago 3 people like this*

Transcript: An Exclusive Interview with Barbara Lagrange

Scene: **Greg Morgan** *stands in front of a series of images depicting the flood damage in Gill Falls, Missouri.*

Greg Morgan: For almost three weeks now we have turned on our televisions and computers and PDAs and found ourselves hearing or reading one name: Melissa Nevis. At first the news was all about her supposed dramatic descent over the Gill Falls Waterfall. Then it was about the efforts by Search and Rescue crews, as well as the many volunteers who showed up unbidden in Gill Falls, to find her body. Then, when it was revealed last week that Melissa Nevis was never in that boat, that she was in fact with her grandmother - Mrs. Barbara Lagrange - the entire time, the conversation shifted to Frank and Victoria Nevis, Melissa's parents, who Barbara Lagrange says asked her to keep Melissa's safety a secret.

Apart from her initial statement announcing Melissa's safety Mrs. Lagrange has been hesitant to speak with the media, and her daughter and son-in-law, Melissa's parents, have offered no statement of their own to explain their actions. Well recently Mrs. Lagrange agreed to speak with the World News Network. Tonight, we will be showing you that exclusive interview.

Scene: **Greg Morgan** *and* **Barbara Lagrange** *sit in armchairs, facing each other.*

Greg Morgan: Mrs. Lagrange, thank you for speaking with us.

Barbara Lagrange: My pleasure.

Greg Morgan: I wonder if you would take us back to that afternoon when your daughter called you and said, I'm assuming, something like, "Mom, would you come pick up Melissa and take her to your house?" Did anything about that strike you as strange?

Barbara Lagrange: It's easy to say now that of course it was strange... I remember offering to pick up all of the children and take them to my house. I don't even... I don't even remember why she said I shouldn't (*laughs*). It just, it just didn't seem that important. I thought something like, well of course Melissa is the youngest and they don't want to have to worry about her, or something like that, but again I didn't think too much about it.

Greg Morgan: But... Come on now... As soon as you saw the news it must have occurred to you what was going on.

Barbara Lagrange: Well I didn't know, you see, I didn't know that what they thought was happening, that Frank had told them Melissa was in that boat. I didn't know anything about it I just assumed that one of the neighbors or someone had thought that Melissa had climbed inside and that was why they were saying she was in there... Again it's easy to say one thing or another about it now but at that time things were very confused.

Greg Morgan: Certainly they...

Barbara Lagrange: I tried to call in to 911 to let them know! I did! You check my phone records, go ahead!

Greg Morgan: And what did they tell you?

Barbara Lagrange: They told me to hold the line, that things were very busy, but that someone would speak to me whenever someone was available to do so. I wasn't going to sit there on the phone just waiting, I knew that nobody was going to talk to me, with all the craziness going on.

Greg Morgan: You mean the flooding.

Barbara Lagrange: Of course I mean the flooding! (*laughs*)

Greg Morgan: (*voiceover*) While we spoke Mrs. Lagrange continued to claim that she knew nothing of her daughter's plans. Mrs. Lagrange does not own a computer, it should be noted, and according to her, she does not typically watch the news. Even still, it seems unlikely that any story that has received such extensive media attention would go unnoticed.

Greg Morgan: So you're telling me you did not know that there was a massive manhunt underway for your granddaughter.

Barbara Lagrange: No.

Greg Morgan: You're telling me that nobody told you that...

Barbara Lagrange: Who's going to tell me? (*laughs*)

Greg Morgan: Mrs. Lagrange you said in your first statement to police that you called your daughter to ask her why everyone thought Melissa had gone over the falls, and she told you to keep quiet about it, and you agreed to do so. Do you remember saying that?

Barbara Lagrange: Sure, I said that.

Greg Morgan: But now you're saying that wasn't true.

Barbara Lagrange: Who knows if it's true? Who knows? (*laughs*)

Greg Morgan: All right, ok, so let's say that somehow you didn't know that all of America was waiting for news about your granddaughter, that people had sent in tens of thousands of dollars in donations, that hundreds of people had traveled to Gill Falls to help in the search, let's say that you were unaware of all of that. Didn't it strike you as odd that Frank and Victoria hadn't asked for Melissa back, that they hadn't talked about picking her up, that they hadn't come to see her?

Barbara Lagrange: No, no, I didn't... I didn't think it was strange, no.

Greg Morgan: How? How could you not think that was strange?

Barbara Lagrange: Because the whole town got flooded! Because they were staying in the shelter with everybody else I figured they just wanted Melissa to stay with me so they wouldn't have to worry about her. I was surprised, I mean if anything was strange I thought it was strange that they didn't send the other kids to come stay with me, that they didn't all come stay with me.

Greg Morgan: All right. All right. I'd like to switch topics a little bit and ask you if you've spoken with your daughter since your announcement.

Barbara Lagrange: I have, I spoke with both her and Frank.

Greg Morgan: And what did they say?

Barbara Lagrange: Oh they just, they apologized to me for putting me in that situation. They said they understood why I did what I did, when I told everybody that Melissa was with me.

Greg Morgan: Did they say anything about what the repercussions of this are going to be?

Barbara Lagrange: I can't, uh, I can't discuss that.

Greg Morgan: *(voiceover)* At the time of our interview charges have been filed against Frank and Victoria Nevis for making a false report to authorities, although we were told that other charges may be forthcoming. No charges have yet been filed against Mrs. Barbara Lagrange for her part in the hoax.

Greg Morgan: What responsibility do you take for all of this?

Barbara Lagrange: All of what?

Greg Morgan: All of this. The media circus and the people driving in and sending in money and...

Barbara Lagrange: The whole shebang?

Greg Morgan: The whole shebang.

Barbara Lagrange: None.

Greg Morgan: None.

Barbara Lagrange: Right. It's got nothing to do with me. I'm the one who put a stop to it.

Greg Morgan: But some people say you're the one who let it go on for as long as it did.

Barbara Lagrange: Who says that? People don't say that.

Greg Morgan: They do.

Barbara Lagrange: Well they're wrong. If I'm guilty of anything I'm guilty of being a good grandmother. That's it, end of story.

Scene: **Greg Morgan** *stands in front of a series of images depicting the flood damage in Gill Falls, Missouri.*

Greg Morgan: During the two hours that we spoke Mrs. Lagrange repeatedly insisted that she was innocent of any wrongdoing. However, authorities may not agree. Shortly after we recorded this interview we received a letter from Mrs. Lagrange's lawyer stating that his client was seeking an injunction against this network that would prevent us from airing the footage you've just seen: not exactly the behavior of someone with nothing to hide. As for Frank and Victoria Nevis, we have yet to hear their side of the story. For World News Network I'm Greg Morgan. Good night.

Either brilliant or completely insane

Meghan Fisher posted a link to her own wall: *www.youtube.com/user/wnn/exclusiveinterivewwithbarbaralagrange?blend=1&ob=5#p/f/2/8c6tcrwwTto 36 minutes ago*

Meghan Fisher commented on her link: This woman is either brilliant or completely insane. *35 minutes ago 4 comments 17 people like this*

DeeDee Millhauser commented on Meghan Fisher's post: Funny how often those two go hand-in-hand... *33 minutes ago*

Patricia Loomis commented on Meghan Fisher's post: I think the whole family is brilliant... This whole thing is obviously some extremely meta performance art piece about celebrity and the state of news-as-entertainment in America... *23 minutes ago 5 people like this*

Tom Rhidel commented on Meghan Fisher's post: @Patricia - I know! I've been saying this for WEEKS, ever since the dad started posting daily updates on you-tube *16 minutes ago*

Patricia Loomis commented on Meghan Fisher's post: @Tom - I know, it was weird, right? *14 minutes ago*

So what do we think about this?

So what do we think about this? Bethany, you had your hand up.

Um yeah I just think it's really sad? You know? That people, that people are willing to do anything to get famous? You know? I mean it seems like they were really just willing to do anything, like they didn't even care that people really thought their daughter was dead.

It's interesting. We understand pretty well when somebody does something for power or for wealth... We are a little bit more ready to accept these as corrupting forces in our lives. We get it when someone sells out their best friend or their spouse for money or power. We may not condone it, but we understand that as a thing that happens sometimes, that power and wealth can do that. We are a little bit less prepared, I think, to see fame in this same light, partially because, even though we think of power and wealth coming with fame, there is something else at work, there's another intangible quality that makes the desire for fame different... Yes, Jeremy?

I don't think it's any different at all. People want fame because fame is power, it's power over people, it's influence, it's everything that power is. I mean, what is power if not influence, and what is fame if not a form of influence?

That's an interesting point. What do we think? Do we think that fame is influence and influence is fame, and nothing more? Jenny.

Uh yeah I don't think that's necessarily the case... Look at all of those "me singing" videos on YouTube... It seems like those people just want to be famous, I mean seen by millions of people... I mean it just seems like they aren't even thinking about what the next phase would even look like if they got famous. It's just the fame itself.

I'm not familiar with the... What is it, "me singing"?

She's talking about there are all of these videos on YouTube of people singing along with pop songs... They record them on their webcams and then post them. A lot of them are completely awful.

Some of them are pretty good.

I mean some of them, but most of them suck. It's perverse.

The other thing about the me singing videos is a lot of these kids look like they're in high school... I mean it's not like they have any concept of the actual economic realities of being an adult, do you know what I mean? I mean I'm sure if you asked any of them they would say that they would love to be rich but more than likely none of them have to pay for their food or their clothes or any of that stuff. What I mean is it doesn't seem like they're doing it so that they can have their big break or whatever, it seems like they just want people to see them. They just want the attention.

Interesting. Ginny, you looked like you were going to say something.

No... Well I was just going to say that when I was a senior in high school one of my friends started posting videos of herself singing on YouTube, and people went nuts. It was so bizarre, it was like Lady GaGa was going to our school. Even the teachers started giving her a break on stuff. Everybody was so sure that she was going to be the next big thing. She was like the queen of the school for the rest of the semester.

Then what happened?

Well then we graduated.

Is she famous now?

Um, no, she's a freshman at Bowling Green.

All right so if we could, let's get back to what Jenny was saying. Do we think that fame is the goal in and of itself, or is it the perks? Joshua?

I mean... What is fame if not the perks? How do you separate one from the other?

Interesting point... There is a school of thought out there that says that people crave fame because what they really want is the existential affirmation of their individual self... The thinking goes that the more depersonalized our society becomes the more deprived we are of necessary social affirmation... We become increasingly isolated, lost in a sort of morass of solipsistic moral relativism which, though it's basically what Nietzsche held as his highest ideal, is actually very hard to handle when you get right down to brass tacks. It's sort of like... Infants who aren't handled when they are very small - children born into institutions and things like this - are at a developmental disadvantage compared to other infants who are handled. We need contact. It is essential to our growth and health and wellbeing, and this school of thought goes that as technology comes to dominate our lives we're left with this unfulfilled need, and that the fame obsession is one manifestation of an attempt to assuage that need. That and... you know, sexual addiction, and people who expose themselves in public... I mean it's all part of the same continuum. Don't you think?

Tonight: Who is Frank Nevis?

You've seen him on the news, you've heard his name, you've prayed for his daughter. But who is Frank Nevis? Tonight, Chad Greeley talks with Jack Liggs, the man who picked up the Nevis family's garbage for the past fifteen years.

Jack Liggs: You can tell a lot about a man by, uh, by what he throws out. (*laughs*)

Tonight, hear the story as told by the only man who can tell it.

Jack Liggs: And I said to him, what are you doing in there? And he just shook his head. He wouldn't tell me.

Tonight, only on The National News Network. Check your local listings.

Gorgon Records, Inc. shared a link...

Gorgon Records, Inc. wrote on their wall: Hey guys check out the new single from Wrath entitled "Father

Don't Make Me," now available on iTunes... Video (audio only, sorry guys no music video yet) is available on You-Tube *30 minutes ago*

Gorgon Records, Inc. shared a link on their wall: *www.youtube.com/user/gorgonrecordsinc/wrath/fatherdontmakeme/watch?v=1b-P0EDGjEE&feature=topvideos_music 29 minutes ago 35 likes 0 dislikes*

Gorgon Records, Inc. shared a link on their wall: *http://www.itunes.apple.com/us/artist/wrath/id136975?ls=1 28 minutes ago 37 likes 0 dislikes*

Wrath shared a link...

Wrath wrote on their own wall: Hey guys check out our new single "Father Don't Make Me," now available on iTunes... *30 minutes ago 45 likes 2 dislikes*

Wrath shared a link on their wall: *http://www.itunes.apple.com/us/artist/wrath/id136975?ls=1 29 minutes ago 47 likes 0 dislikes*

J.R. Burris shared a link...

J.R. Burris shared a link on his wall: *www.youtube.com/user/gorgonrecordsinc/wrath/fatherdontmakeme/watch?v=1b-P0EDGjEE&feature=topvideos_music 14 minutes ago*

J.R. Burris shared a link on his wall: *http://www.itunes.apple.com/us/artist/wrath/id136975?ls=1 13 minutes ago 3 likes 0 dislikes*

J.R. Burris commented on his post: This song is F#CKING AMAZING *12 minutes ago*

Father Don't Make Me (Single)

Song: **Father Don't Make Me**
Artist: **Wrath**
Album: **Father Don't Make Me** (*Single*)
Label: **Gorgon Records, Inc.**

Father don't make me
Father don't make me
The floodwater's rising
The floodwater's rising

I can't, I won't, I just abide
I can't, I won't, I'll run and hide
The floodwater's rising and the time is near
The floodwater's rising like a young girl's fear

Father don't make me
Father don't make me
The floodwater's rising
The floodwater's rising

Father I know that you had your dreams
That now they're lost, I know it seems
Like the water is rising now just for you
But it isn't so, it isn't true

Father don't make me
Father don't make me

The floodwater's rising
The water is rising

As strong as a current is the lie that you told
It's as wide as the river, and deeper and cold
It's washed over us all, we're all held underneath
We can't fight against it, we can't even breathe

Father don't make me
Father don't make me
The floodwater's rising
The water is rising

Father don't make me
Father don't make me

Tonight: Who is Frank Nevis? (Part 1)

You've seen him on the news, you've heard his name, you've prayed for his daughter. But who is Frank Nevis? Tonight, Chad Greeley talks with Jack Liggs, the man who has picked up the Nevis family's garbage for the past fifteen years.

Jack Liggs: You can tell a lot about a man by, uh, by what he throws out. (*laughs*)

Tonight, hear the story as told by the only man who can tell it.

Jack Liggs: And I said to him, what are you doing in there? And he just shook his head. He wouldn't tell me.

Tonight, only on The National News Network. Your news coverage starts now.

Scene: **Chad Greeley** *stands in front of a picture of a flood-damaged street in Gill Falls.*

Chad Greeley: Good evening. The report you are about to see is a NNN exclusive. Jack Liggs has been a city employee in Gill Falls for twenty years. For the past fifteen years his duties have included sanitation work in the areas including the quiet street on which the Nevis family lives. What does this mean? He collects their garbage and as he will tell you, sometimes what people throw out tells you more about them than what they keep.

Scene: **Chad Greeley** *and* **Jack Liggs** *sit in armchairs, facing each other.*

Chad Greeley: Good evening.

Jack Liggs: Good evening.

Chad Greeley: I wonder if we could just start with you telling our viewers your general impressions of the Nevis family.

Jack Liggs: Uh, sure, they were... Uh, I don't know, nice enough people I guess.

Chad Greeley: Nice enough people.

Jack Liggs: Sure.

Chad Greeley: Gill Falls is a town of nice people.

Jack Liggs: Sure. Definitely. It's, you know, your standard small town. (*laughs*)

Chad Greeley: I think one of the reasons that people are so surprised by this whole situation, with Frank and Victoria telling everyone that their daughter went over the waterfall and then it turning out that she hadn't, that they had staged the whole thing...

Jack Liggs: Uh-huh

Chad Greeley: ... is that these are such nice, typical, small town people. Or at least...

Jack Liggs: Sure.

Chad Greeley: ... at least that's the perception.

Jack Liggs: Right.

Chad Greeley: But that's not your perception.

Jack Liggs: Well, see, with what I do... I get a chance to get to know people in a way that other people don't. (*laughs*)

Chad Greeley: You mean by picking up their trash.

Jack Liggs: By picking up their trash.

Chad Greeley: So tell us, what did you find that made you say to yourself, these people, the Nevises, they aren't just like every other family on this block. These aren't just your average, small-town-America folks.

Jack Liggs: You wouldn't believe it.

Chad Greeley: (*voiceover*) When we return, the shocking truth behind the Nevis family's small-town facade.

Me Singing "Father Don't Make Me" by Wrath

Fay Moynahan posted a video on YouTube: *Me Singing "Father Don't Make Me" by Wrath 20 minutes ago*

User Comments:

LOL oh my god you SUCK why do people post these? FIREKING1 *13 minutes ago*

@FIREKING: omgstfu!!!! @FAY: i think you sound GREAT don't let idiots stop you from doing what you love!!!!!

PATTYV67 *10 minutes ago*

Fay Moynahan posted a link on her wall: *www.you tube.com/user/fayallday/fatherdontmakeme/watch?v=1b-P0EDGjEE&feature 19 minutes ago 2 comments 4 people like this*

Fay Moynahan commented on her post: Hey guys check out my video *18 minutes ago*

Todd Bodder commented on Fay Moynahan's post: I love these keep posting you sound GREAT!!! *8 minutes ago 1 person likes this*

Fay Moynahan (*@fayallday*) tweeted: Hey guys check out my new video me singing father don't make me http://bit.ly/iMyRHS *16 minutes ago*

Tonight: Who is Frank Nevis? (Part 2)

Chad Greeley: (*voiceover*) We've been speaking with Jack Liggs, city worker in Gill Falls, Missouri, the man who, for the past fifteen years, has picked up the Nevis family's garbage. As Mr. Liggs tells it, a person's garbage can tell you a lot about them.

Jack Liggs: I'm not saying what they threw away was strange, I'm just saying it wasn't the sort of things that most people threw away.

Chad Greeley: What sort of things?

Jack Liggs: Oh, all sorts of things. I mean, parts, spare parts from things. Blueprints and stuff like that.

Chad Greeley: The sort of thing you might expect to find in an inventor's garbage. Failed experiments, that sort of thing.

Jack Liggs: Sure.

Chad Greeley: What sort of things were these inventions?

Jack Liggs: I couldn't say. I mean, everything that came out was smashed up or broken. I mean, that's why he was throwing it away! (*laughs*)

Chad Greeley: Sure, sure. But what I mean is, did you get any sense, was there any sort of theme to these inventions? Were they all, say, kitchen appliances, or home goods, or robotics? Could you...

Jack Liggs: I'm sure I wouldn't know the first thing about what any of it was for or what any of it did. Like I said, it was all pretty broken up. There was one thing one time that I thought was a... I mean it sort of looked like it had been made out of a vacuum cleaner, it had hoses coming out of it and I thought for a second that it was like a vacuum cleaner with more than one nozzle, so like two people could vacuum at the same time. That was one thing that I sort of thought I could figure out... Other than that everything was... uh, it was unrecognizable.

Chad Greeley: Let me ask you a different question. You picked up the Nevis family's garbage every week.

Jack Liggs: That's right.

Chad Greeley: Every week there's a new invention in the trash?

Jack Liggs: No, I mean not every week.

Chad Greeley: But there are pieces. What I mean is there is evidence that Frank Nevis has been working on something.

Jack Liggs: Sure, that's probably accurate. It seemed like that. I mean looking back on it it seems like there was always something.

Chad Greeley: Now we know that for the past almost seven years Frank Nevis has been working two jobs to support his family, to support Victoria and Melissa and the other children. Mr. Liggs you have a family, am I correct?

Jack Liggs: That's right I have two daughters.

Chad Greeley: And you work full-time as a city employee.

Jack Liggs: That's correct.

Chad Greeley: How much time do you have to spend with your family when you get done with work at the end of the day?

Jack Liggs: Sheesh. Not as much as I'd like, that's for sure. (*laughs*)

Chad Greeley: In your opinion, someone working a full-time job and another part-time job, he's got to have almost no time with his family, and you're telling us that every week there is evidence that Frank Nevis is out in his garage trying to invent a new... vacuum cleaner or whatever.

Jack Liggs: I suppose.

Chad Greeley: What does that say about what kind of father Frank Nevis is?

Chad Greeley: (*voiceover*) When we come back, the conclusion of my interview with Jack Liggs, stay tuned to NNN.

You searched for: me singing "father don't make me"

Your search for *me singing "father don't make me"* produced 43 results

Title: **Me singing "Father Don't Make me"**
Uploaded by: RichInSpirit *45 minutes ago*
Duration: 3:03
345 views / 12 likes / 35 dislikes
Description: Me Singing "Father Don't Make Me" by Wrath... sorry I have a little bit of a cold but someone requested that I put this one up... Thanks for watching!

User Comments:

nice you sound just like them maybe you should hit puberty and get some friends and never post anything like this ever again
DROPKICKDAVID *29 minutes ago*

@DROPKICKDAVID: LOL
MIKED67 *23 minutes ago*

Title: **video of me singing "Father Don't Make Me" by Wrath**
Uploaded by: TruthBombs24 *41 minutes ago*
Duration: 3:12
120 views / 2 likes / 3 dislikes
Description: I love this band and I love their new song... hope you enjoy!

User Comments:
REALLY REALLY BAD LOL
VINCEMCCOY *40 minutes ago*

thats mean vince but seriously you arent good please stop posting these thank you - the entire youtube community
HARRYCURRY4 *36 minutes ago*

NICE job man f the haters you should be famous no seriously i think your better that the guy from wrath which isnt saying much because that band is awful
NICKYFROMTHECITY *33 minutes ago*

this video makes me wish i was born deaf
DEVOMYWEAVO *29 minutes ago*

Title: **video of me singing "father don't make me" by wrath**
Uploaded by: MyamiHeat *20 minutes ago*
Duration: 3:02
45 views / 3 likes / 10 dislikes
Description: sorry guys i no the mic sux im trying to get a betr 1 hope you njoy all the same!!!! luv!!!

User Comments:
I mean this from the bottom of my heart, and believe me I'm usually the last one to say this, but seriously you need to go back to school, because you are kidding yourself if you think you can sing.
DJJeremy *18 minutes ago*

i agree with djjeremy... take an online course or something... get an associates degree in filing... do anything other than this
GUNit8 *15 minutes ago*

This video is digital pollution
DBLDEKKER *12 minutes ago*

Tonight: Who is Frank Nevis? (Part 3)

Chad Greeley: Did anything strange ever happen when you were picking up their garbage?
Jack Liggs: There was one time I remember, we pulled up outside their house and it was about five or five-thirty in the morning, and I seen somebody standing out by the curb waiting for us. So I get down off the truck and I call out, you know, "Hey," you know, "Good morning."

(*laughs*) Then the guy comes over, and I seen that it was Frank Nevis so I says, "Good morning, Frank," and he says good morning, and he tells me he's got something he wants to get rid of but that he can't move himself, and would I mind coming and helping him move it.

Chad Greeley: He wanted you to come inside and help him carry it.

Jack Liggs: Right.

Chad Greeley: I see. Go on.

Jack Liggs: So I follow him into the garage and first of all, you can barely walk in there, there's so much stuff all over the floor.

Chad Greeley: What sort of stuff?

Jack Liggs: Oh all kinds of stuff. Just odd and ends, you know, mechanical pieces.

Chad Greeley: I see. Go on.

Jack Liggs: We get over back in the corner and he's got this thing all uncovered and pulled out, like he tried to move himself and then had to stop. And... and I'm looking at this thing and I have no earthly idea what it is. (*laughs*) So I say, you know, "Frank, what the heck is this thing?" you know? And I said to him, "What are you doing in there?" And he just shook his head. He wouldn't tell me.

Chad Greeley: Could you describe what it was to our audience?

Chad Greeley: (*voiceover*) Mr. Liggs' description of the object went on for longer than we have time to share with you, but we had him sit down with a police sketch artist who composed the rendering you now see on your screen. We showed this drawing to several research scientists at UCLA and none of them would make any guess as to what purpose such an item might have served, though some of them felt that, owing to several of the features that Mr. Liggs described, the item was of dubious scientific merit.

So who is Frank Nevis? The question, perhaps, is better expressed as, Who are any of us? Is it possible for us to know another's mind and if so, what was going on in Frank Nevis's mind on that stormy night, when he told the authorities that his daughter was being carried away by the rising flood? We may never know. Repeated requests for an interview made to the Nevis family from this network and several of its affiliates went unanswered, and our telephone calls were not returned. For the National News Network, I'm Chad Greeley. Goodnight.

Before we play this song, we just want to say

Thank you everybody for coming out! This song, this song we're about to play is brand new and the single just came out what was it Friday, guys? It came out last Friday, you can get it on iTunes and you can go on our Facebook page and hear it... Anyway this is our brand new song... And, uh, before we play this song, we just want to say... A lot of you know I'm sure about Melissa Nevis... Um, the whole situation out there is just, it's just crazy, I don't know if you guys have been watching the news or anything but this little girl, her father is this really sick individual... He told everyone that she had been carried off by the flooding that was happening in their town this was in Mississippi or was it... oh no right it was in Missouri, my bad... But anyway he told everybody that she had been carried off and over this waterfall but it turns out the whole time he had hidden her at her grandmother's house... Anyway the band, we heard this story and we started talking about it and we were thinking about how... There are a few experiences that happen to you when you're a little kid that stick with you, and we were talking about the first time we could remember our parents lying to us... And then we were saying, do you remember the first time one of your parents asked you to lie for them... It's a pretty fucked up thing for a little kid, right? When one of your parents asks you to lie for them? So we were thinking about that a lot when we wrote this song... This is *Father Don't Make Me*.

Other Voices from Gill Falls, Revisited

Title: **Other Voices from Gill Falls, Revisited**
Uploaded by: GTOGuy *19 hours ago*
Duration: 5:22
36,991 views / 3,451 likes / 4 dislikes
Description: During the media circus before, during, and after the "Gill Falls Girl" hoax, the residents of Gill Falls have been trying to put their lives back together. If you ACTUALLY care about helping out, you can make donations to the Gill Falls Chamber of Commerce www. GillFallsCC.com.

Scene: *The living room of a house, a young woman is pulling up carpet.*
Camera Operator: So what are we doing here?
Young Woman: Well I'm tearing up the carpet because it's, uh, because it's ruined, of course. I mean naturally it's ruined. So we're going to tear up the carpet and then see how bad it is underneath, and what we have to do about that. I don't know. This is the first time I've been back,

since they told us we could come back. This... I don't know.

Camera Operator: You haven't been back at all?

Young Woman: Uh, no, I... I went and stayed with my brother in Ohio and I kept hearing from everybody here that there were tons of people coming into town to help out and I just... It just sounded like a madhouse to me. There's nobody here now, though.

Camera Operator: Do you think that everybody left when they heard that Melissa Nevis wasn't really... that she didn't really go over the waterfall like everybody thought she did?

Young Woman: I...

Camera Operator: I mean, like, do you think they just lost interest because...

Young Woman: No, I know what you mean. And... I mean, there's nobody here now, so... You know? I mean, I could say no, but if not then... where are they?

Scene: *Interior of a tent. A young man is sitting on a sleeping bag.*

Camera Operator: So can you tell us where we are?

Young Man: Uh, sure, we're here in my tent, and I've got it set up in my parents' backyard while I'm helping them clean up the house.... They, you know... I told them that nobody was going to come take anything, you know, that everything is just a fucking wreck in there, that there's nothing to take (*laughs*) but... uh, I guess they're still just worried so I told them I'd sleep out here and keep an eye on the place for them.

Camera Operator: So... have you guys had any help from anybody, I mean, putting things back together and everything? Cleaning up?

Young Man: I mean... everyone around here is just trying to clean up their own, you know their own mess (*laughs*)... You know everybody's got plenty to do on their own.

Camera Operator: What I mean is has anybody come in from... from you know outside of the town to help?

Young Man: Oh ok yeah, I mean some folks are coming in from some of the towns around here... There are a few people from a church over in Tipply that I seen for the past couple of weekends but, uh, not like in the first few days after the flood.

Camera Operator: Do you think that people stopped coming, do you think that people stopped coming out to help after they found out that Melissa Nevis didn't really go over the waterfall?

Young Man: No, no I don't think so. I mean that was what, like ten days after the flood? People were already... Well, no, I guess there were still people... I don't know, I didn't think about it in terms of.... in terms of that. But no, I don't think... I don't think people would... People who would come out to help would come out to help one way or the other, you know? People who would come and help strangers are good people, they don't need a big story or a... you know a thing like that to make them come out.

Camera Operator: So you think people just... you think people just lost interest?

Young Man: I don't know. I mean... Everybody's got their own things, you know? You know, I mean, who are we to say that we're any worse off than any of them? Everybody's got... you know they've got their things to deal with. God puts things in front of everybody, you know. I'm grateful for... for the time that people did spend here. I mean nobody had to come out at all, but they did. That's what I focus on. I don't try to focus on the, you know the rest of it, why they aren't here now.

Scene: *A group of people, mostly middle-aged, sit under a tree eating sandwiches.*

Camera Operator: So I guess what I'm trying to... to get people to talk about is you know like... what kind of help people are giving you guys right now, like if there's a lot of help coming in from outside.

Middle-aged Man: I don't know... Jerry, you want to take that one?

Jerry (another middle-aged man): I... uh... (*laughs*) I'm not sure you want to record what I have to say about it.

Others: Come on, tell him.

Jerry: I better not say anything. No, no.

Others: Aw, boo!

Camera Operator: What? What is it?

Jerry: All right, all right. (*laughs*) Ok so I was over working on the retaining wall along the river, you know where all of those railroad ties got washed away. We were digging out the bank and then putting in new ties and then backfilling the rest. I had like six kids from this church over in... I don't know somewhere over... I don't remember where, somewhere just over the border in Iowa. They'd all driven in because their pastor told them to or something. Anyway I came back from, I don't remember... I had to run over and get some more shovels or something, and when I came back these kids were gone. Just - whoosh! - gone just like that.

Camera Operator: Where did they... I mean where did they go?

Jerry: I don't know, home I guess. I guess they just decided they had better things to do.

Camera Operator: When was that?

Jerry: Oh, I don't know. Few days ago. Eight or ten days ago.

Camera Operator: Was it the day that... that Melissa's grandmother came out and said that Melissa was with her the entire time?

Jerry: Uh... well? Maybe? I'm not sure. When was that?

Others: No, it was, it was!

Jerry: Well, I guess there's your verdict.

Scene: *The interior of a firehouse. One fireman is talking to the Camera Operator.*

Camera Operator: So how's it coming, with all of the cleanup and everything?

Fireman: Are you kidding me? It fucking sucks, man. It SUCKS. (*laughs*)

Camera Operator: (*laughs*) But I mean, are you making progress? I mean is it coming along or... or what?

Fireman: I don't know. I guess so. It was coming along a lot faster when we had all of those people here, I'll tell you that.

Camera Operator: You mean the volunteers who were coming in and helping.

Fireman: Uh-huh. I mean, I get it, that now that Melissa didn't go over the waterfall it isn't quite as... whatever, I don't know, hip or something to come help us out but we still need help. (*speaks close in to the camera*) You hear me, America? (*laughs*) We need help! (*laughs*) I don't want to do all of this shit by myself.

Camera Operator: (*laughs*) So you think... You think that people stopped coming when they found out that Melissa... that she didn't actually get taken over the falls?

Fireman: I mean... Don't you?

Superimposed white text on black background: The people of Gill Falls, Missouri have a monumental task before them. They need your help to get their lives back to normal. It is wrong to hold an entire town accountable for the actions of one family. If you want to help, donations can be made to the Gill Falls Chamber of Commerce at www.GillFallsCC.com. Or come visit... *fade in on image of flooded Main Street with superimposed text:* Just remember to bring your waders.

User Comments:
What is happening in Gill Falls is not only wrong, it is un-American. It is so sick that we only care about our neighbors when there is some scandal to gawk at, and not when they actually need our help.
HARVYtheCAT *15 hours ago*

@HARVYtheCAT: I assume, then, that you're writing your comments from Gill Falls, where you are waist-deep in the relief efforts...
STELMOSFIRE23 *15 hours ago*

@STELMOSFIRE23: I am 67 years old and confined to a wheelchair... Though it is none of your business I have made a contribution to the Gill Falls Chamber of Commerce, as suggested in the video... Maybe you should consider that you don't know everybody's circumstances before you start making smart-ass comments
HARVYtheCAT *15 hours ago*

@HARVYtheCAT: my bad just assumed with a stupid user name like harvythecat you were some self righteous fourteen-year-old girl... my mistake lol
STELMOSFIRE23 *14 hours ago*

Hey everyone thanks for watching... You can check out my other videos on my youtube channel youtube.com/user/gtoguy... thanks and god bless all of you who are making donations after watching!
GTOGuy *14 hours ago*

@HARVYtheCAT: so what's your better idea? that we spend hundreds of thousands, probably millions of dollars in federal relief funds to fix up Gill Falls? that we raise taxes everywhere so that ma and pa Gill Falls can get their feed store back in tip top shape? theres a name for that sort of thing... SOCIALISM.
LIVEFREEorDIE *13 hours ago*

You are all obviously incapable of intelligent discourse. I will not be replying to any further comments.
HARVYtheCAT *12 hours ago*

And here they are, performing their new single

...And here they are ladies and gentlemen, performing their new single *Father Don't Make Me*... it's Wrath!
.... And thank you very much just wonderful, wonderful, love the new song. So tell us a little bit about it I understand that there's sort of an interesting, an interesting, uh, story behind why you all came up with that, uh, that song, why don't you tell us a little bit about it.

Uh, sure, thanks yeah, and thanks for having us on. Um, yeah, the new song is sort of, or well it's inspired by, I don't know if... Does your audience know about what happened in Gill Falls, with the flooding and with the little girl...

Sure... sure... Oh, yep, sounds like they know about it.

So, yeah, so her name is Melissa Nevis and I guess your audience already knows the story but to I guess anyone at home who doesn't know, when the authorities started telling people to evacuate this girl's parents they sent her to stay with her grandmother who lived like, I don't know, fifty miles away or something...

...Well out of danger of the flooding.

...Right way away from the flooding and then when the flood came her parents had this boat in their garage that I guess the father had been working on and the boat got carried away and went over the waterfall, and the girl's parents told everybody that she, the little girl was in it.

...And the idea was that this way they would get a lot of attention and sympathy and...

...Right I mean... I guess that's what the idea was.

So anyway you were telling me a little bit, before the show, you were telling me that this story, this story of this little girl, struck a very personal chord with you all why don't you, uh, why don't you tell us a little bit about that.

Oh ok sure well we were all watching updates on this story on the bus and we started thinking... I mean we're all children of divorced parents and we started sort of saying oh, yeah, you remember the first time you had to lie to one parent to cover for the other, and pretty soon we really started feeling for this little girl, feeling like we sort of understood what that was like for her, having to lie for her parents basically by hiding and going along with this basically this lie that her parents were telling the whole country basically.

I see so you really... You felt like you could really empathize with what this little girl, with what Melissa Nevis was going through.

Right, sure. And we just wanted... I mean our music, all of our music is about trying to tell these kids, I mean we meet these kids at these shows and they're all made up and dressed up but they're still just little kids, you know? And they have this look in their eyes where you can just see that nobody where they're from, nobody in their high school or at home can understand what they're going through, and these kids think they're all alone. And so when we play, the songs we write we're just trying to say, you know, you're not alone. There are people out there who know how you feel, and it's ok, you know? Like, you're ok, and you're going to be ok.

Well powerful, powerful stuff and like I said, love the band, love the new single... The song is called *Father Don't Make Me* and the band is Wrath... I want to thank you guys for coming on.

Thanks for having us.

Thanks also to Cameron Diaz, and sorry to Gerard Butler we will have to get you on the next time you're in town. From everyone here, good night!

The Nevis Family Speaks

Title: **The Nevis Family Speaks**
Uploaded by: FrankNevis *1 hour ago*
Duration: 2:12
111 views / 2 likes / 45 dislikes

Description: The Nevis family breaks their silence for the first time since their daughter Melissa has been home.

Hi... So this is me, Frank Nevis, and I'm here with my wife Victoria and the kids... Say hi guys... A lot of people have been asking us to do interviews and to talk about what has been going on with us and we... um, we haven't felt ready... We thought it was more important to focus on being a family again and to try to get our home back, put back together after the flooding... As you can see we've made some progress but, uh, but the place is still kind of a wreck.... Yeah I just... I don't know. But anyway we felt like everybody wanted to know and so we thought... that... uh... that we owed it to people to give some explanation... And the other thing is that it seemed like people had really already made up their minds about us and on the one hand we really wanted to come out and reply to these things people were saying about us and on the other hand we knew that there just... that it wasn't going to do any good if everybody already thought they knew what had happened so Victoria, my wife Victoria said why don't we wait, you know, wait a little bit and then tell our side when people are ready to hear it. So, uh, we're going to be posting another video in the next couple of days just saying what it was like, you know, on our side of the situation and just let everybody know that, you guys don't know everything that was going on and so, don't, uh, don't jump to any conclusions about us. Ok.

User Comments:
Correct me if I'm wrong, but this is basically a teaser trailer for the video that he's saying they're going to put out in the next couple of days?!? this guy is fucking ridiculous.

BATWING56 *55 minutes ago 34 likes*

@BATWING56: your not wrong that is exactly what this is this whole thing would be brilliant if it wasn't so sleazy
GABERUDEBOY *54 minutes ago 23 likes*

Maybe he's right... maybe we shouldn't jump to any conclusions.... LOL
TIPPYHEADRUNNER *46 minutes ago 3 likes*

The Nevis Family Speaks

Title: **The Nevis Family Speaks**
Uploaded by: FrankNevis *2 hours ago*
Duration: 2:12
5,121 views / 4 likes / 451 dislikes
Description: The Nevis family breaks their silence for the first time since their daughter Melissa has been home.

The Nevis Family Speaks

Title: **The Nevis Family Speaks**
Uploaded by: FrankNevis *3 hours ago*
Duration: 2:12
124,345 views / 7 likes / 1,234 dislikes
Description: The Nevis family breaks their silence for the first time since their daughter Melissa has been home.

The Nevis Family Speaks

Title: **The Nevis Family Speaks**
Uploaded by: FrankNevis *4 hours ago*
Duration: 2:12
789,902 views / 19 likes / 3,811 dislikes
Description: The Nevis family breaks their silence for the first time since their daughter Melissa has been home.

The Nevis Family Speaks

Title: **The Nevis Family Speaks**
Uploaded by: FrankNevis *5 hours ago*
Duration: 2:12
1,253,221 views / 21 likes / 5,761 dislikes
Description: The Nevis family breaks their silence for the first time since their daughter Melissa has been home.

In a video message that quickly went viral

...Well breaking news tonight out of Gill Falls, Missouri where the Nevis family has finally broken their silence. In a YouTube video message that quickly went viral Frank Nevis, father of Melissa Nevis - the so-called "Gill Falls Girl" - and the subject of an investigation into possible criminal misconduct, explains that the family has not come forward to tell their side of the story because they felt that people had already formed an opinion about what happened. Though he does not go on to say what that side of the story is in the video, he does promise that another video will be posted in the next couple of days in which he will explain what actually happened. Now you can find that video, as well as more on all of our breaking stories on our website, www.MyNews37.com where you can also subscribe to our podcast and sign up for our daily email updates on the stories we are currently following...

Frank Nevis Breaks Silence, Doesn't Say Much

by Daniel Thrush, guest contributor

Gill Falls, MO - In his long-awaited reply to the various insults, complaints, and accusations being lodged against him, Frank Nevis took to his webcam Monday night to say... not much of anything.

With his wife and children by his side Frank Nevis explained that he had been waiting to break his silence until he felt that "people were ready to hear" his side of the story, saying that he was reluctant to speak sooner for fear that "people had really already made up their minds" about what happened. His side of the story, however, went untold, as the video concludes with Nevis promising that he will post a second video "in the next couple of days."

The video comes a full three weeks after the flooding in Gill Falls in which Nevis claimed that his 6-year-old daughter, Melissa, was carried over the Gill Falls Waterfall in an experimental watercraft of Nevis' own design. It comes eleven days after the revelation that in fact Melissa was staying with her grandmother, Mrs. Barbara Lagrange of Headon, MO, during the entire incident. Since that time both Nevis and his wife Victoria have been charged with making a false report to authorities, though further charges are pending.

Daniel Thrush is a frequent contributor to the Halliford Sentinel Online. Contact Daniel directly at DThrush@ HallifordSentinel.com.

Paul Fuller wrote...

Paul Fuller wrote on his own wall: A year from now Frank Nevis is either going to be in jail or have his own reality show... *24 minutes ago 6 comments 15 likes*

Harry Mills comment on Paul Fuller's post: or both lol *23 minutes ago*

DeeDee Fitch commented on Paul Fuller's post: I agree with Harry i would love to watch a reality show about frank nevis in prison... that would be quality entertainment *21 minutes ago*

Dick Cooper commented on Paul Fuller's post: i know right? this whole thing is either ridiculously stupid or totally brilliant... guess we'll see which one it is a year from now! *14 minutes ago*

Rich Yanchich commented on Paul Fuller's post: 1 yr from now jail, 2 yrs from now talk show, 3 years from now bestselling book (ghostwritten), 4 years from now replaces Regis Philbin, 6 years from now congressman / house rep. only in america *10 minutes ago*

Dick Cooper commented on Paul Fuller's post: @Rich: LOL! USA! USA!

Gene Fielding commented on Paul Fuller's post: @Rich: you're probably right... I shudder to think what that same timeline will look like for Melissa... *7 minutes ago*

What Else Is Going On in the World?

And now we turn to Rudy Greene for a segment we like to call, *What Else Is Going On in the World?* Take it away, Rudy!

Thanks Jen! Well busy week all over the globe as protests and violence and the threat of violence have all escalated all across the Middle East! Israeli and Palestinian leaders have been unable to reach any sort of agreement in their most recent dispute! Food shortages have led to riots in Tunisia and Egypt, and Yemen is on the brink of civil war! In Cannes, this week officials rolled out the red carpet for celebrities arriving for its annual film festival, and some of Hollywood's hottest stars were in attendance! In Nigeria, the Human Rights Watch has estimated that eight hundred people have been killed in post-election rioting, and it looks like country music star Kenny Ford and his wife Loretta are expecting another baby! That's all the time we have for *What Else Is Going On in the World?* I'm Rudy Greene... Jen, back to you!

So Mr. Nevis, you must be pretty relieved

The Saturday Night Show
Show # 28
Musical Guest: Wrath
Sketch Title: "Gill Falls Girl"

Characters:
        Grace Powers [a newswoman]
        Frank Nevis
        Victoria Nevis
        Melissa Nevis
        Other Nevis Children

[Open on GRACE POWERS, standing in front of a house. Wind and storm effects.]

GRACE POWERS:
Good evening I'm coming to you tonight live from Gill Falls, Missouri where in the midst of flooding and torrential storm conditions, one family is fighting their own private and heartbreaking battle with Mother Nature.

[Enter FRANK and VICTORIA NEVIS]

FRANK NEVIS:
Our poor baby! Oh what will we do? Our daughter is being carried down the river in that boat which you cannot see into and will surely be taken over the falls!

VICTORIA NEVIS:
Oh God, if You can hear me, save our little girl!

GRACE POWERS:
[She is standing beside MELISSA NEVIS, who has entered during her parents' lamentations.]
Um... But isn't this Melissa?

MELISSA NEVIS:
Hi mom, hi dad.

[FRANK and VICTORIA fall to their knees and embrace MELISSA, the whole time glancing uncomfortably at the camera and jockeying for a better sightline.]

FRANK NEVIS:
Oh, thank God you're all right! How awful it would be if something happened!

VICTORIA:
That's right! I'm going to make sure nothing can ever happen to you; I'm going to take you and put you in the evacuation bus right now! [She takes MELISSA's hand and leads her offstage]

GRACE POWERS:
So Mr. Nevis, you must be pretty relieved that your daughter is all right.

FRANK NEVIS:
[With a disappointed look] Yeah, I guess.

[VICTORIA NEVIS reenters, frantic]

VICTORIA NEVIS:
She's fallen down a well! Melissa has fallen down a well!

FRANK NEVIS:
[Excitedly] She has? I mean [Concerned] she has? Oh no! When will our trials end?

GRACE POWERS:

But Mr. and Mrs. Nevis, isn't that Melissa? [She points through the window of the house, where we can see Melissa playing]

FRANK NEVIS:
[Glancing awkwardly at the camera] So it is! Oh thank God! I'll just go and get her and make sure nothing else happens to her! [Exits]

GRACE POWERS:
Well Mrs. Nevis, a harrowing day for you to say the least! First you think your daughter has been carried off in a boat, then you think she's fallen down a well! And we know that you really believed these horrible things, because you told everyone, and not just everyone in the town, but everyone in America! [Indicates the camera and audience.]

VICTORIA NEVIS:
Oh, well, yes [She begins brushing her hair to look better on camera] Well I know all of the mothers out there will understand the kind of hardship you suffer when you think that your child is in danger!

[FRANK NEVIS emerges from the house, his hands covered with blood.]

GRACE POWERS:
Oh my God! Mr. Nevis! What happened?

FRANK NEVIS:
There's been a terrible accident! Melissa is dead!

VICTORIA NEVIS:

She is? [She and FRANK clasp hands and for a moment start to jump up and down in celebration, then they remember the camera and try to look sad.]

GRACE POWERS:
But Mr. and Mrs. Nevis, isn't this your daughter Melissa? [She is now holding MELISSA's hand.]

[FRANK and VICTORIA look at Melissa, then at each other; FRANK looks at the blood on his hands in obvious confusion.]

VICTORIA NEVIS:
How... I mean how...

GRACE POWERS:
Well that's all the time we have... For Channel Six News, I'm Grace Powers saying...

[A rowboat floats past in the foreground, containing the OTHER NEVIS CHILDREN.]

OTHER NEVIS CHILDREN:
Hi mom, hi dad, wheeeeee! We're going for a ride over the waterfall!

FRANK and VICTORIA NEVIS:
Kids! [They run offstage after the boat]

GRACE POWERS:
Well it certainly has been an exciting day here in Gill Falls. For Channel Six News I'm Grace Powers, good night.

Over-eager and irresponsible digital permutations

There is a lesson to be learned from the so-called "Gill Falls Girl" incident, but it is almost certain to be a lesson ignored by those that could most benefit from its wisdom. I am speaking, of course, of the news media, and all of its over-eager and what can only be called irresponsible digital permutations.

When the floodwaters rose above the hastily-built and temporary retaining wall set up along the river banks television news crews, along with an assortment of their new-age, digital counterparts (bloggers, tweeters, and the like), were already on the scene, anxiously awaiting the arrival of disaster. Read that sentence one more time: they were *anxiously awaiting the arrival of disaster.* Many of you, I'm sure, find nothing amiss: what's wrong, you ask, with news reporters arriving to report the news? I don't claim that there is anything wrong with reporting the news; what I do wish to suggest is that when news organizations work to report in *anticipation* of the news, they are in effect doing something very closely related to publicity work. Again, perhaps you see nothing wrong with this, but if you do then I urge you to consider the ramifications of this subtle shift.

When I was a child there were five television stations and two news shows. News happened and it was reported to us by the anchor, an unwaveringly avuncular man whose even tone assured us that, despite whatever had happened, we were all still here and still all right. There was little if any "live" news coverage: that was reserved for planned speeches and events simply by virtue of the immobility of broadcasting and video recording equipment. The advent of the portable video camera, however, made it possible for the reporter to travel into the field (in the same way that a print reporter would) and report *from the scene*. This advancement was followed quickly by the advent of the satellite truck, and soon there was almost no pause between news occurring *live* and the news being reported. Couple this with a burgeoning cable news field and suddenly you have real and heated competition among newscasters to get on the scene and report first.

The question arises, however, as to whether this immediate reportage is of substantive value. Often, we know, immediacy begets a lack of information or worse, the presence of misinformation, which when reported (in the newscaster's haste and need to provide content with the cameras rolling) passes into the vague limbo of reported but unverified truth. This is the antithesis of news reporting, and does more to confuse the public than it does to inform them. So why is this the standard model for every modern-day news agency?

The answer, of course, is viewership. The irresistible allure of reality, of potential disaster, of the still-smoldering embers far outweighs whatever value we, as a viewing public, ascribe to the facts of the situation. In essence we watch live news to experience a voyeuristic and vicarious thrill - *in exactly the same way we consume other forms of entertainment.*

Don't misunderstand me: the news shows of my youth were still shows, and everything about them was designed to lure viewers away from the competition. Better ratings meant (and still mean) more and better advertising, and that means - then as now - more money. But the news itself - the content of the program - was somewhat insulated from this effect: the news was the news, and the "show" aspects of the news show were expressed solely in the broadcast's form. (You may argue that there is always a hand - sometimes well-obscured and sometimes graceless and obviously visible - directing the content of the news: which stories are reported, which are given a few minutes more, etc. I will not dispute this: as I said, the news shows of my youth were still shows. I do assert, however, that there was a level of journalistic respect for the story itself holding an intangible but no less powerful barrier between reportage and showmanship. It is this barrier that I fear has been eroded to the point of non-existence, much to our detriment.)

And so, you ask: what is the danger in courting viewership? How much harm is there, really, in reporting on a story before the facts are all in, with the understanding that more facts will become available in the future, and will be reported then?

The question becomes: what is the function of the news media itself? If we take it for granted that now news is only entertainment then perhaps there is no danger at all: if news is so constant and uninformed as to lose credibility, then we can all sleep soundly in the knowledge that this misinformation has no real world consequence. Sadly (or perhaps not sadly, depending on your feelings on the matter) this is not the case, and the viewing public still depends on the news for the *facts* on which they will base their own judgements: judgements which do carry ramifications in everything from social justice to politics to the brand of mustard being used in school lunches. What we have, in effect, is a clumsy and unintentional propaganda machine, in which any wild and unverified claim can (for a few hours at least) linger in the dangerous realm of suggestion and rumor: unsubstantiated, it is no less influential. Smear campaigns, contaminations scares: these are symptoms of a system so dependent on instant content that it will eat whatever it is fed. There simply is no time for consideration, sourcing, fact-checking; no time, in effect, for journalism.

But even this is less troubling than the subject of this article. So let me return, briefly, to the muddy banks of the Gill River, and the news personnel anxiously awaiting the disaster.

There is a phenomenon in research science known as "data dredging" in which researchers skew their result data to reflect their preconceived notion of the likely outcome. Drug companies have a tremendous economic incentive to show that their new product does what they hope it will; a graduate student, facing down the day when he or she will have to make his or her case before the assembled faculty of his or her chosen discipline, has little time for error (and little leeway, in fact, for the kind of surprising discoveries that the process of experimentation is designed to foster). In these cases the financial repercussions of failure are only part of a larger aversion: the stigma of incompetence or ignorance looms large, and it is not at all surprising that we find ourselves, if not coloring, then at least shading the truth somewhat in our own lives (to ourselves and to our peers) so that we may dismiss this specter and continue to regard ourselves approvingly (and merit our peers' continued approval as well).

I knew a woman once who, as she grew older, began to put on weight, and took to weighing herself in an effort to track and hopefully quell this trend. However, as the weeks went by and the scale continued to reflect advances in the wrong direction, she began to mentally quantify the weight of her most recent meal and subtract it from her total, with the theory that the food in her digestive tract was keeping the scale from reflecting her "true" weight. As she continued to gain, the imagined weight of her previous meal began to grow accordingly, so that by the time she finally stopped and joined a weight-loss program, she told me, she was regularly telling herself that she'd somehow managed the miraculous task of eating somewhere between twelve and fifteen pounds of food, and so could not be held accountable for that weight, and could maintain the delusion that her "true" weight was constant and, if not ideal, then at least familiar.

The point of that story is that data dredging is not relegated only to the laboratory or to the halls of academia: these little lies we tell ourselves are part of a seemingly natural function of our fallible egos, and as such define our experience with their pervasive and enticing campaign. We *want* to believe certain conclusions, even when the data is not there to support our claims.

But you are undoubtedly wondering what this has to do with the brief history of broadcast journalism, the news personnel anxiously awaiting the disaster on the banks of the Gill River.

When Frank and Victoria Nevis told the authorities that their daughter was being carried away by the rising flood they did so with a kind of brilliant (if perhaps only instinctual) savvy: we do not know, as of yet (as the Nevises have so far refused all interviews), the premeditation that preceded this fraud, but we do know the instant repercussions - we do know that the story was picked up by news outlets across the country, that almost before the vessel that was supposed to have held Melissa Nevis slipped over the falls her name had been heard by hundreds of thousands - if not millions - of people. The Nevis' lie crossed the threshold into, if not truth, then something very like it, for nothing more than the cost of telling it. This could only have happened in the current climate of news speculation, in which newscasters are seeking out disaster and calamity, so much so that - like the woman lying about her true weight - their perception becomes colored by their desire.

The "Gill Falls Girl" situation is the most recent and among the most glaring examples of the failures of the current system. An environment in which the effort of news gathering relies upon a large degree of speculation and postulation, in which anchor and story have become inexorably linked, in which the voracious appetite of the twenty-four hour news cycle demands constant content will always be susceptible to the flaws inherent to such a situation, the most perplexing among these being the platform's susceptibility to misinformation and the likelihood that then this misinformation will be disseminated to a broad audience. Again, if we assume that news has crossed the threshold into entertainment then there is no danger in this misinformation being spread: it is of little concern or consequence if the wrong name is given for the accused or the deceased. If, however, we agree that the news still functions as news, then it becomes imperative that these organizations uphold their responsibility to the public and present only those facts that can be properly sourced and vetted - in short, must present only those facts that have had time to present themselves, and must therefore give up the frantic kind of reporting that seems to be today's standard. I humbly suggest a return to the predominance of desk and anchor.

Dr. David Sellers is the professor of Media and Cultural Studies at Whitlock College. His work has appeared in The New York Times, the New Yorker, The Atlantic Monthly, and The Virginia Quarterly Digression. He is a frequent contributor to this magazine.

Did anybody hear?

Tom Young posted on his own wall: Hey, did anybody else hear that Frank Nevis is going to be interviewed on NNN tonight? I thought I heard it while I was flipping through the stations but they might have just been talking about him, not saying they were going to interview him... *17 minutes ago 4 comments*

Grady Brown commented on Tom Young's post: I thought I heard something about that too... I feel like it would be a bigger deal you would hear about it more if it was really happening tho... *12 minutes ago*

Bill David commented on Tom Young's post: I looked it up after I read your post yeah he's going to be on with Greg Morgan http://www.wnn.com/gregmorgan/interview /franknevis *10 minutes ago*

Carl Nero commented on Tom Young's post: That guy is such a douche I hope Morgan tears him a new one *7 minutes ago 3 likes*

Bill David commented on Tom Young's post: yeah and check this out if you aren't already thoroughly disgusted by this guy... just found this. http://www.you tube.com/franknevis/thenevisfamilyspeakspart2/watch?v= I9tWZB7OUSU&feature=related *1 minute ago*

The Nevis Family Speaks - Part 2

Title: **The Nevis Family Speaks - Part 2**
Uploaded by: FrankNevis *1 hour ago*
Duration: 0:54
239 views / 2 likes / 200 dislikes

Description: The Nevis family breaks their silence for the second time...

So hi everyone just me this time and it's just going to be a quick video I just wanted to let everyone know that Greg Morgan who some of you may know who has an interview show on WNN is going to have me on... Uh, I'm going to go on Greg Morgan's show that's going to be tomorrow night at seven PM on the World News Network... Uh, so I'm going to talk to him and you can all tune in there and then I'll post a video in the next few days with my wife, with both Victoria and I and... and I know that Melissa has something she wants to say to all of you. So tune in tomorrow night... and, uh... and then check back here. Ok.

User Comments:
This family in unbelievable... there are no words for what these people are doing.
HappyGOLucky23 *55 minutes ago*

@HappyGOLucky23: I think the word you're looking for is reprehensible.
HITCHIYAYA *50 minutes ago*

@HITCHIYAYA: or brilliant.
KafkaInManhattan *49 minutes ago*

@KafkaInManhattan: or REPREHENSIBLE.
HITCHIYAYA *46 minutes ago*

@HITCHIYAYA: I just mean that the way Frank Nevis has exploited the publicity-gaining capabilities of the new media and leveraged it into traditional public-

ity, i.e. an interview with Greg Morgan, is kind of remarkable. I'm not condoning it, I'm just saying it's impressive.
KafkaInManhattan *43 minutes ago*

FUCK TONIGHT!!!!! Meet hot local singles!!!! Our nationwide database will HOOK YOU UP!!!!! Click here: www.hdiwia.com
JCASHMONEY *38 minutes ago*

@KafkaInManhattan: all of frank nevis's tactics are sleazy and manipulative, and if we feed into them and watch his interview and everything else we are just feeding into a trend where anyone who wants to be famous will bombard us with content all the time... the internet is going to look like an alley full of panhandlers
HITCHIYAYA *37 minutes ago*

@HITCHIYAYA: isn't that how it looks already?
KafkaInManhattan *34 minutes ago*

WORK FROM HOME MAKE $500/HOUR FILLING OUT INTERNET SURVEYS EASY MONEY! www.MakeMeMoney.com
FREEMONEYGIVEAWAY *33 minutes ago*

Tonight! On Greg Morgan

---

http://www.wnn.com/gregmorgan/interview/franknevis

Tonight on the World News Network, Greg Morgan sits down for the exclusive interview America has been waiting for. Frank Nevis has maintained his silence. Tonight he talks with Greg Morgan, live. Tonight, only on the World News Network. Check your local listings.

www.GillFallsGirlTees.com

www.GillFallsGirlTees.com

Welcome to Gill Falls Girl Tees Online, your one-stop shop for apparel related to the Gill Falls Girl Hoax! All of our tee-shirts are 100% cotton and printed in the USA, and NONE of the money goes to Frank or Victoria Nevis! What could be better? Show your friends your lighter side with a humorous or ironic Gill Falls Girl Tee! Thanks for looking, and God Bless!

Featured Items:

Tee-Shirt Reads: *My Dad told everyone that I went over a waterfall, and all I got was this lousy tee-shirt!*
100% cotton preshrunk tee
Available in Small, Medium, Large, and Extra Large
Colors: White, Navy, Red, Black
Printed in the USA
$22.95

Tee-Shirt Reads: *Gill Falls Girl Groupie*
100% cotton preshrunk tee
Available in Small, Medium, Large, and Extra Large
Colors: White, Navy, Red, Black

Printed in the USA
$22.95

Tee-Shirt Reads: *Visit the Gill Falls Waterpark! Where you don't go on any rides, but you tell everyone that you did.*
100% cotton preshrunk tee
Available in Small, Medium, Large, and Extra Large
Colors: White, Navy, Red, Black
Printed in the USA
$22.95

Tee-Shirt Reads: *Gill Falls Levee Buster*
100% cotton preshrunk tee
Available in Small, Medium, Large, and Extra Large
Colors: White, Navy, Red, Black
Printed in the USA
$22.95

Tee-Shirt Reads: *I [HEART] Gill Falls Girl*
100% cotton preshrunk tee
Available in Small, Medium, Large, and Extra Large
Colors: White, Navy, Red, Black
Printed in the USA
$22.95

Tee-Shirt Reads: *Gill Falls Search & Rescue*
100% cotton preshrunk tee
Available in Small, Medium, Large, and Extra Large
Colors: White, Navy, Red, Black
Printed in the USA
$22.95

Tee-Shirt Reads: *I [HEART] Melissa Nevis*

100% cotton preshrunk tee
Available in Small, Medium, Large, and Extra Large
Colors: White, Navy, Red, Black
Printed in the USA
$22.95

Tee-Shirt Reads: *Visit beautiful Gill Falls, MO: Where the river comes to you.*
100% cotton preshrunk tee
Available in Small, Medium, Large, and Extra Large
Colors: White, Navy, Red, Black
Printed in the USA
$22.95

Tee-Shirt Reads: *Nevis Vacation Planners: Enjoy Gill Falls, Leave the Kids in Headon*
100% cotton preshrunk tee
Available in Small, Medium, Large, and Extra Large
Colors: White, Navy, Red, Black
Printed in the USA
$22.95

Live Tonight: the Exclusive Interview

Good evening. A little more than one month ago disaster struck the small town of Gill Falls, Missouri. The Gill River, swollen by unusually heavy rains, crested its banks and flooded the town of 4,800, destroying businesses and residences, causing hundreds of thousands of dollars worth of damage. Residents couldn't have predicted on that terrible day that the devastation caused by the floodwater would soon be overshadowed by another story, one that would eventually shake this small town to its core and leave residents wondering if any of them really knew the people living next door. I'm Greg Morgan, and tonight I'm joined by Frank Nevis, the man behind what many are now calling the "Gill Falls Girl Hoax." Tonight we are coming to you live with the interview that you have been waiting for. Mr. Nevis, good evening.

Good evening, Greg. Uh. Hi.

Mr. Nevis let me ask you the question that I think America has been waiting to ask and that is, What do you have to say for yourself?

I, uh, well I don't have anything to say for myself.

No apology? No explanation?

Apology? Apology to who?

Well, how about to the hundreds of people who came out to Gill Falls to help with the cleanup, after they heard about your tragedy? How about the thousands of people who sent money -

Why should I apologize to them?

Because they feel misled... Because you misled them.

I don't... uh... I don't know about all that... I mean if you ask those people they may tell you that we... You know that what Vicki and I did had something to do with it but I bet you'll find that nobody came out to help who wasn't, uh, you know, wasn't already the kind of person who was going to come out and help, or was going to send money... I mean I'm sorry that they felt misled, if that's what you want me to say, but I mean really they still did a good thing which is, uh, which is what they were trying to do, wasn't it?

Well then how about an apology to the Search and Rescue crews that risked their safety to search for your daughter? Or to the taxpayers who are going to have to pick up the bill for it? Or to the people - excuse me, you'll have a chance to answer - or to the people who were up on that bridge, trying to snare the boat before it went over the falls? You don't feel that you owe any of them an apology?

I don't feel... I mean I'm not going to apologize to them but that's because they're all suing me. I don't... uh... I don't know what you want me to say. I deny all wrongdoing, as far as that's concerned.

All right. Why don't you... Why don't you tell us what the plan was? Why you did this?

I... uh, I mean... Why I did this. It was just a... a prank, you know? It was a stunt.

A stunt?

Yeah, it was a publicity stunt.

A publicity stunt.

Right.

I think the thing we're all thinking is that... Uh, that with most publicity stunts there are no consequences. Nobody risks their lives or... or sends in money. What you did is closer to fraud. In fact, it might be worse than fraud.

I don't... Oh, come on. Nobody spends their money? That's the whole point of a publicity stunt, is to get people to go and spend money.

But they have a choice... It isn't just... A publicity stunt is there to create the desire for a product or a show or a service... It isn't just a ploy for money.

Mine wasn't a ploy for money! I mean... that's what mine was, what you're describing, that's what it was. I didn't... nobody sent me any money. None of the money came to me, the money all went to charities that are doing good things in Gill Falls, trying to rebuild all of the stuff that got damaged.

So you're saying that, uh, you're saying that your, I guess we're calling it a publicity stunt now, that your publicity stunt was just like any other, that it was there to promote some product. That's what you're saying.

That's what I'm saying.

Mr. Nevis, and I hesitate to ask this, what product are you promoting?

Well I'm promoting me!

You? You're promoting yourself?

Yes. Yes, I am promoting myself.

I'm not sure that I... I mean that... I'm not sure that I understand how you're thinking you're promoting yourself. I mean I'm not sure of, uh, in what capacity you're thinking that you've been... uh, I mean how is this promotion going to manifest or what are you trying to get it to manifest into? I mean what do you think is going to come of this?

Anything. Any and everything. I am completely open to whatever comes my way. Life is about saying "yes" to possibilities, Greg.

Is that how you saw what happened with your daughter? Was that you saying "yes" to an opportunity?

Of course. Naturally. Opportunity was knocking.

Because...

Because everyone was paying attention. News vans started pulling into town hours before the evacuation order even went out. Everybody's attention was on us.

And so you said, This is my chance for people to know the name Frank Nevis.

Correct. Correct, correct, correct.

All right. All right we'll get back to that in a moment. For now, why don't you tell me how Melissa and your other children are handling all of this. You and Victoria have five children, is that correct?

Yes, uh, Sandra is eleven, Billy is ten, June is eight, Tommy is seven, and of course Melissa is six.

Eleven, ten, eight, seven, and six. How are they handling all of this? What is a day at school like for your children? Do the other kids give them a hard time?

I... Why would the other kids give them a hard time?

I don't know. Maybe because of things they've heard their parents say about you and Victoria, maybe because of things they've heard, I don't know.

No, nobody is giving them a hard time.

And if I brought them out here and asked them the same question, do you think they'd give me the same answer?

Why wouldn't they?

I don't know. Because it seems unlikely to me that, uh, that there hasn't been any sort of backlash after this incident from your neighbors. I just think that's... uh, frankly I find that unbelievable.

No... Why is that so unbelievable? We've lived in this town for, I mean we've known all of these people for years. My kids have lived in Gill Falls their entire lives.

I... I'm not going to disagree with you, but I am going to say that I find it completely fantastic that your neighbors aren't ready to drive you out of town on a rail. I mean that's a fantastic notion to me. If you look... I mean your name is all over the blogosphere and Facebook... People are reviling you. They're saying your children should be taken away from you, that you are a hazard to your family, that you and your wife are so obsessed with fame that you're willing to put your children at risk...

I never... hey! I never put my kids at risk. Melissa was more out of harm's way than anyone when the flood happened.

She was certainly more out of harm's way than those people on the bridge who thought they were saving your daughter's life. I mean, you have to agree with me there.

Those people were certainly in harm's way. What do you have to say to them?

I... look. I'm not stupid, ok? I did research on the Search and Rescue protocols in this kind of situation. Our house, you've seen our house, on the news and wherever. Our house is right on the river. I knew that as soon as the boat got out onto the river the Search and Rescue crews weren't going to risk trying to go get it, which is exactly what they did, and they told everyone else not to go after it either. Those people up on the bridge, I mean I'm, I'm grateful to them for what they thought they were doing, you know trying to pull the boat back and everything, but they were going directly against what Bill Brixley, you know Bill Brixley the Fire Chief, what he told them to do. I mean I'm sorry that Sarah Carter injured her hand but I mean she should have done what the evacuation personnel told her to do.

So, just for the viewers at home, you feel no responsibility for those injured.

I... I feel sympathy for them, I mean I'm sorry in that way, that sort of thing, but I can't be held accountable for what people decide to do, when everyone has told them not to.

All right. Let's go back, I want to go back for a moment to what you said earlier. You're here, you're open for business, you're the product. Am I getting you? You are what you are trying to promote with the, uh, with this prank? I'm sorry this, uh, this publicity stunt?

That's right.

So... What does that mean? I mean without going into your full... your full pitch or anything... I think people at home are wondering what sort of a... a goal could motivate someone to do something like this. What did you see happening? What did you think was going to come of this?

This.

This?

This! This... What's going on right now. Me sitting here talking to you. My YouTube videos getting more than a million hits... Did you see? The other night they had a thing on The Saturday Night Show about us. Somebody sat down and wrote a script with characters Frank and Vicki Nevis.

So... Fame? So you just... wanted to be famous?

Yes! I mean... no, but not *just* famous. I mean you say that like famous is just famous and that's it.

But that's not it.

No, of course that's... Come on, Greg. Come on. Famous is just famous? You know what I'm talking about, you're a famous guy. Famous is just famous? I don't think so.

So what is it?

It's *everything*. It's... If you're not famous in this country then who are you? Nobody.

You're whoever your friends and your family and your neighbors...

Don't give me that. You're nobody, and everybody out there, everybody watching knows what I'm talking about. Nobody just wants to be another nobody just sitting out in some little nothing town watching the TV and trying to ignore how bored they are, they want to be *on* the TV. They want to be the ones everyone else is watching.

You want to be the one everyone else is watching. Maybe I'm not understanding you, but what do you think... I mean what do you imagine you're going to feel like when you are on the TV, and everyone else is watching you, now? I mean, how do you feel right now? There are millions of people watching you right now. Do you feel... I mean do you feel how you thought you would feel? Did you get what you wanted?

Well... I mean NO, obviously... Not yet... I mean right now everybody in the country is mad at me and suing me and I have people writing letters to the Governor saying that my kids should be taken away and that I'm a danger to my family... And I mean I can't go back to my home I mean people can be, I mean they are, they are mad at me and I get that but people either forgot or they don't care that everybody who lost their home in that flood, you know, we did too. We lost our home, too. We're still flood victims, we still don't have anything to go back to, we're staying right now we're staying with Vicki's sister in Iowa. So... yeah. So that's it. I don't know what people want me to say. Our lives are destroyed. How about a little sympathy?

I think people feel like you manipulated the sympathy they had for you, and that's why they don't feel sorry for you anymore.

Well... I mean that's their... uh, that's their decision I guess.

All right. So tell me. One year from now. It's one year later. Tell me, in your mind, what does your life look like? What has come of all of this?

Well... uh, hopefully my show gets a second look...

By your show you mean... uh, let me see, you mean *The Invention of Family*?

That's right.

Ok so let me stop you briefly and have you tell the folks watching at home what that show, what *The Invention of Family* was or, I guess, what it is.

Sure, uh, *The Invention of Family* is a reality show that we made a few, uh, a few years ago with the Continental Cable Company and the idea was that a camera crew would sort of stay with us, with Vicki and the kids and I, and it would film us as we did all of the normal family stuff but it would also document my inventions and, you know, follow me as I tried to get them patented and... and you know follow us to trade shows and meetings with retailers as, um, as the inventions started selling, that sort of thing. And we... we filmed a pilot, we got the funding to film a pilot and we shot it and then... Then we didn't hear back for a while, then somebody told us they were going to do it, then we didn't hear anything for a while, then they said they were looking at it for next season... You know how these things go.

So, one year from now, *The Invention of Family* is in production, you're inventing, you're back in your... I take it you're back home?

Well... Maybe not back home. I mean if the show got picked up we could afford to move I guess and with the insurance money and... I don't know. I'm, uh, I'm not sure they want me back in town anyway.

So somewhere else.

Sure. Somewhere else.

And your family would be all right with this? They would go along with this, this being on this show and moving from the town, your children have lived in Gill Falls all their lives, correct?

Uh, yes that's correct.. uh, the kids love the show. They loved being in the pilot, it was all I heard for weeks after, Daddy daddy, when are the cameras coming back, daddy daddy when are we going to be on TV?

So your children want to be famous, too?

I don't see... When you're famous everybody... everybody loves you. Even the people who hate you love you, because they're all looking at you. That's love. That attention that people give you. Nobody pays any attention to you unless you're famous. Nobody cares what you do or what you've done. So, I mean, why wouldn't my children want to be famous?

Children get that attention from their parents. That's supposed to be the way it works. You're telling me that your children want to be famous because they don't get enough attention, that nobody cares what they do?

Don't put words in my mouth. Don't make it sound like... Don't... That's not what I'm saying. I'm saying that in the world, in you know in society today, if you aren't somebody then you're nobody. That's all I'm saying. Some people don't mind! Some people don't mind being nobody, but I mind, and Vicki minds, and our kids, even though maybe they don't understand it the way Vicki and I do, you know, because they haven't been out in the world, and seen how people can be, they still get it, you know, they still *know*. I mean all little kids want to be what? Girls want to be princesses and singers and boys want to be superheroes because why? Because they get it. No little kid sits around pretending to be an audience member, you know? No little kids sits around dreaming about being a servant to the princess, they want to *be* the princess!

All right Mr. Nevis we're running out of time but before we go, let me ask you if there's anything you want to say to the people out there, to anyone you may have hurt or misled, or maybe you don't feel like you've, uh, like you've hurt or misled anybody but if there's anything you want to say?

Uh... I guess just that... Just that I don't think I'm all that different from most people... You know? I'm just a normal guy, I love my family, I want good things for my family. I don't think that I... that I did anything anyone else wouldn't have done, just maybe I was in the right place at the right time to do something. I guess. I mean people... people are lied to every day of their lives. They don't care. They get told, you know, uh, that things are one way, you know? That reality shows aren't scripted and that game shows aren't fixed, things like this. They're happy to believe whatever story they get told because it's all just... it's all just a show, isn't it? I mean isn't it? You're in TV, Greg, you tell me. Did we get the whole story on nine eleven, or did we just get enough of it to make us think that we had to go to war?

Mr. Nevis I think we're getting a little off the subject...

No, I mean I'm not trying to get off the subject, this is the subject, isn't it? The media telling us what's going on is the subject. What's one more lie? I mean what's the biggest fault here, is it that I did it in the first place or that I didn't pull it off? If Melissa had stayed with her grandma and been raised in Headon and nobody ever found out all of those people out there who tried to do something good would go on living thinking that they'd done what they thought they did, do you understand what I'm saying? Truth is just... is just whoever is telling the story the loudest, and the people with the cameras and the blogs and the news shows like this one are...

But you're saying that what we do, what journalists do, is... Well actually I don't know what you're saying, either you're suggesting that we make up stories or that we... I don't know that we somehow falsify the stories to make them more... more what? More deceptive? For what?

You tell me, Greg. Advertising, political power...

All right this is getting a little bit...

Who do you think your boss is having dinner with right now? Who do you think your boss is having dinner with right now?

I... Well... I have no idea, Frank. Why don't you tell me who you think he's having dinner with.

I don't know but I'll tell you one thing for sure, it isn't some little nobody like me. It isn't some little small town nobody, it's some powerful executive like him with lots of eggs in lots of baskets, and sooner or later he's going to say to your boss, Oh, it looks like this one story you're going to cover would be bad for this basket that I've got some of my eggs in, so why don't you do me a favor buddy and not run that story? Or change the name of the basket? Or leave out the name of the basket? Would you do that for me buddy?

I see so in your mind the media is a... is a vast conspiracy keeping the true news veiled behind a screen of... what would you call it would you call it misinformation to affect the viewing audience's opinions to the benefit of those controlling it?

Exactly.

Mr. Nevis please.

What?

Please. Are you hearing yourself? This doesn't sound a bit far-fetched? Look I've worked in television for many, many years, and nothing in television is that organized. For crying out loud, I mean it's hard enough to find a cup of coffee on this floor.

All right, Greg. All right, viewers at home. Hi, viewers at home. Go to sleep, buy our brand-name products! There's no man behind the curtain! Frank Nevis is the bad guy, the news is the good guy, don't worry, everything is going to be fine...

All right that's all the time we have. I'd like to thank our producers and the crew here at the World News Network studios in New York. I'd also like to thank Frank Nevis for agreeing to do this interview. Thank you, Frank.

Thank you, Greg.

From all of us at WNN, I'm Greg Morgan saying, goodnight.

Well that was different

Hello and welcome to The Daily Dish, your one-stop-shop for all the latest in celebrity and pop culture news, and the biggest story this morning can be told in two words FRANK NEVIS in an interview with WNN's Greg Morgan last night Nevis touched on just about everything from the strangely insightful to the paranoid and bizarre; let's take a listen.

"When you're famous everybody... everybody loves you. Even the people who hate you love you, because they're all looking at you. That's love... Did we get the whole story on 9/11, or did we just get enough of it to make us think that we had to go to war?... I never... hey! I never put any of my children at risk..."

Wow well *that* was different. Now there has been no further comment from the Nevis camp since the live interview was broadcast last night, but stay tuned as we bring you all the latest...

...And just when you think the buzz is going to start dying down, it kicks right back up again. Last night Frank Nevis, the man responsible for the now notorious "Gill Falls Girl" prank sat down with WNN's Greg Morgan, and he had this to say:

"I have people writing letters to the Governor saying that my kids should be taken away and that I'm a danger to my family... I never put my kids at risk. Melissa was more out of harm's way than anyone when the flood happened... I mean I'm sorry that Sarah Carter injured her hand but I mean she should have done what the evacuation personnel told her to do... I'm saying that in the world, in you know in society today, if you aren't somebody then you're nobody. That's all I'm saying. Some people don't mind! Some people don't mind being nobody, but I mind, and Vicki minds, and our kids, even though maybe they don't understand it the way Vicki and I do, you know, because they haven't been out in the world, and seen how people can be, they still get it, you know, they still know."

In the one-hour interview Mr. Nevis explained that the dramatic events surrounding his daughter's alleged trip over the Gill Falls Waterfall during the flooding a month ago were part of an elaborate plot designed to draw attention to Mr. Nevis and his family in the hope that it would revive a defunct reality show, once optioned to the Continental Cable Company, now a part of the Global Entertainment Industries Conglomerate, centering on the Nevis family and Mr. Nevis's passion for scientific experimentation and invention. Now a pilot for the show was filmed, but the series was not picked up for production. Only time will tell if Mr. Nevis's ploy will pay off, but with public opinion turning south by the minute it seems unlikely that any network will risk bankrolling the Nevis family. Now we will have more on this story as it develops.

Frankophile

by Bob Tucker, Staff Writer

New York City, NY - It has been more than a month since the notorious "Gill Falls Girl" incident, but it looks like the story may just be getting interesting. In an interview with World News Network's Greg Morgan last night Frank Nevis revealed that all of the attention the media has been paying him and his family has been the point all along. In statements that pundits have characterized as everything from eloquent to delusional Mr. Nevis described his plan to gain attention for his failed reality show, while simultaneously dissecting the current state of the new media:

"[The] truth is... just whoever is telling the story the loudest," said Mr. Nevis, who went on to explain that those loudest voices were owned by "the people with the cameras and the blogs and the news shows."

While most have dismissed these statements as the rationalizations of a guilty man, there are some who see them as something more.

"He's a genius," says 25-year-old Molly Fischer. "He sees the way things are so clearly."

Molly is the driving force behind *Frankophile,* a Facebook group and blog devoted to all things Frank Nevis. As of this writing the group had only 135 members, a number which Ms. Fischer insists is growing daily.

"People have been looking for someone like [Frank Nevis]," she explains. "The world is getting crazy. There are thousands of voices shouting at us all the time, from our computers and our televisions and newspapers and telephones. Frank Nevis cuts through all of that."

The Facebook page and blog are like a scrapbook of the events surrounding the "Gill Falls Girl" stunt / hoax / prank. Links and still images populate the wall, and blog entries are typically limited to explanations of what viewers will find by clicking on other links. Still, Ms. Fischer insists that her site offers more than searchers would find on their own.

"Our members are really interested," she says. "We search this stuff out. We don't have just what you're going to find if you Google search for Frank Nevis. We get out there and we look around."

As for Mr. Nevis himself, one wonders how he will react to his newfound celebrity. There are numerous examples - in the era of "reality entertainment" - of people publicly and grandly getting what they wish for, only to find out that all that glitters is not gold. Still, talking to Ms. Fischer, one gets the sense that Frank Nevis may have, whether inadvertently or intentionally, set his finger on the pulse of some intangible groundswell, some cultural phenomenon in search of a figurehead. For now, this reporter will just have to wonder, as calls to Mr. Nevis were not returned.

But even as I stop to consider how fame will treat Frank Nevis, it occurs to me that perhaps I am only caught up in Ms. Fischer's enthusiasm, that in all likelihood I am overestimating the staying power of a novelty celebrity like Nevis', or overestimating his ability to leverage it to his advantage. After all: it has only been a month, and only time will tell if the name Frank Nevis will stick or slide, whether his story will become another half-remembered media circus in which the events remain in the mind but the names have all but disappeared.

As this thought occurs to me - as I am folding up my notebook and preparing to leave our interview - a small "bloop" sounds from Ms. Fischer's laptop.

"All right," she said, clapping her hands. "We just got another member. From 135 to 136. Now we're really on our way."

Bob Tucker is a Staff Writer for the Daily Dispatch-Chronicle Online. Contact Bob directly at RobertTucker@Daily DispatchChronicle.com. A subscription to the print version of this newspaper is available at www.daily dispatchchronicle.com/print/subscriptions. Molly Fischer's group Frankophile can be found on Facebook. com at www.Facebook.com/group/Frankophile. The Frankophile blog may be found at www.Frankophile.blog host.com.

Ryan King posted on his own wall

Ryan King posted on his own wall: watching Frank Nevis get interviewed is like watching surgery... I'm repulsed and fascinated at the same time *13 hours ago 5 comments 14 likes*

Jen Alpern commented on Ryan King's post: I know! It's like a car wreck... It's horrible and I know that people are suffering, and yet somehow I can't look away... *12 hours ago 2 likes*

Sarah Bishop commented on Ryan King's post: That guy is reality TV gold... I can't imagine why they didn't pick up the show about him and his family *11 hours ago*

Ryan King commented on his own post: @Sarah Bishop: totally! I can't wait until they pick it up (which they are definitely going to do)... I could watch him spew crazy 24/7 *10 hours ago 2 likes*

Hillary Guffman commented on Ryan King's post: I like how Greg Morgan basically didn't do anything to stop him from looking completely batsh*t crazy... Sign of a true professional *10 hours ago*

Ryan King commented on his own post: @Hillary Guffman: exactly... give 'em enough rope... *9 hours ago 3 likes*

Frank Nevis Interview (Full)

Title: **Frank Nevis Interview (Full) - Part 1**
Uploaded by: FlyGirl *19 hour ago*
Duration: 9:46
78,289 views / 289 likes / 234 dislikes
Description: Full interview Frank Nevis's interview with WNN's Greg Morgan part 1 of 4

Title: **Frank Nevis Interview (Full) - Part 2**
Uploaded by: FlyGirl *19 hour ago*
Duration: 9:34
68,982 views / 231 likes / 123 dislikes
Description: Full interview Frank Nevis's interview with WNN's Greg Morgan part 2 of 4

Title: **Frank Nevis Interview (Full) - Part 3**

Uploaded by: FlyGirl *19 hour ago*
Duration: 8:55
23,098 views / 123 likes / 432 dislikes
Description: Full interview Frank Nevis's interview with WNN's Greg Morgan part 3 of 4

Title: **Frank Nevis Interview (Full) - Part 4**
Uploaded by: FlyGirl *19 hour ago*
Duration: 9:55
49,083 views / 534 likes / 927 dislikes
Description: Full interview Frank Nevis's interview with WNN's Greg Morgan part 4 of 4

See more results like this

Title: **Frank Nevis interview highlights**
Uploaded by: MagnaCartaMistake *13 hour ago*
Duration: 4:45
12,394 views / 123 likes / 32 dislikes
Description: Some of Frank Nevis's greatest hits... Please "like" if you enjoy this video, and check out my other videos

See more results like this

Title: **I'm Promoting Me (The Frank Nevis Interview SOng)**
Uploaded by: AutoTuneYourMom *3 hours ago*
Duration: 2:46
93,823 views / 23,923 likes / 2 dislikes
Description: During the flooding in Gill Falls, Missouri, local resident Frank Nevis told authorities that his six-year-old daughter Melissa had climbed into an experimental boat that had been kept in the garage of the

family's home, and that that boat was subsequently taken by the floodwaters and carried over the Gill Falls waterfall. This claim was later revealed to be untrue, and Frank Nevis to be the author of one of the greatest pranks perpetrated on the public in recent history. Now, after weeks of silence, he is dropping some knowledge.

See more results like this

Gabe Tressler shared a link

Gabe Tressler shared a link on his own wall: *www.you tube.com/user/autotuneyourmom/impromotingme(thefrank nevisinterviewsong)?blend=1&ob=5#p/f/2/8c6tcrwwTto 5 2 hours ago 4 likes*

Gabe Tressler commented on his own post: This is the funniest shit I've seen in years. *2 hours ago*

Derrick DeYoung shared a link on his own wall: *www. youtube.com/user/autotuneyourmom/impromotingme(thefr anknevisinterviewsong)?blend–1&ob=5#p/f/2/8c6tcrwwT to 5 2 hours ago 6 likes*

Hannah Russel shared a link on her own wall: *www. youtube.com/user/autotuneyourmom/impromotingme(thefr anknevisinterviewsong)?blend=1&ob=5#p/f/2/8c6tcrwwT to 5 2 hours ago 2 likes*

Jake Mills shared a link on his own wall: *www.you tube.com/user/autotuneyourmom/impromotingme(thefrank nevisinterviewsong)?blend=1&ob=5#p/f/2/8c6tcrwwTto 5 1 hour ago 15 likes*

Bobby Whick shared a link on her own wall: *www.you tube.com/user/autotuneyourmom/impromotingme(thefrank*

I'm Promoting Me (The Frank Nevis Interview SOng)

Title: **I'm Promoting Me (The Frank Nevis Interview SOng)**
Uploaded by: AutoTuneYourMom *15 hours ago*
Duration: 2:46
1,923,293 views / 293,972 likes / 2 dislikes
Description: During the flooding in Gill Falls, Missouri, local resident Frank Nevis told authorities that his six-year-old daughter Melissa had climbed into an experimental boat that had been kept in the garage of the family's home, and that that boat was subsequently taken by the floodwaters and carried over the Gill Falls waterfall. This claim was later revealed to be untrue, and Frank Nevis to be the author of one of the greatest pranks perpetrated on the public in recent history. Now, after weeks of silence, he is dropping some knowledge.

(Greg Morgan)

Mr. Nevis, good evening
Mr. Nevis let me ask you
Mr. Nevis, good evening
What do you have to say say?
What do you have to say?
What do you have to say say?
What do you have to say for yourself?

(Frank Nevis)

I'm promoting me! Yes
I'm promoting me!
I'm promoting me! Yes
I'm promoting me!
Life is about saying "yes" to possibilities, Greg, Greg,
Greg, Greg.
Life is about saying "yes" to possibilities, Greg, Greg,
Greg, Greg.
I never... hey! I never put my kids at risk.
I never... hey! I never put my kids at risk.

I'm not stupid, Greg, Greg.
I'm not stupid, Greg.
I'm not stupid, Greg, Greg.
I'm not stupid, Greg.

(Greg Morgan)

Your children want to be famous, too?
Good evening, Mr. Nevis.
Your children want to be famous, too?
Mr. Nevis please.

(Frank Nevis)

If you're not famous then who are you?
Nobody no nobody
If you're not famous then who are you?
Don't put words in my mouth.

If you're not famous then who are you?
Nobody no nobody
If you're not famous then who are you?

Everybody loves you.

(Greg Morgan)

Mr. Nevis please please
For WNN, I'm Greg Morgan
Mr. Nevis please please
For WNN, I'm Greg Morgan saying

(Frank Nevis)

Go to sleep, buy our products!
Frank Nevis is the bad guy
Go to sleep, buy our products!
There's no man behind the curtain!

I don't think I'm all that different.
I'm just a normal guy,
Go to sleep, buy our products!
Frank Nevis is the bad guy
I don't think I'm all that different.
I'm just a normal guy,
Go to sleep, buy our products!
Frank Nevis is the bad guy

I'm not stupid, Greg, Greg.
I'm not stupid, Greg.
I'm not stupid, Greg, Greg.
I'm not stupid, Greg.

(Greg Morgan)

I'd like to thank our producers and the crew here at the World News Network studios in New York. I'd also like to thank Frank Nevis for agreeing to do this interview. Thank you, Frank.

(Frank Nevis)

Thank you, Greg.

User Comments:
This video is FUCKING HILARIOUS
BALLS2theWALL247 *13 hours ago*

super funny thanks guys for posting...
HITIMES7 *11 hours ago*

Frank Nevis needs help... his obsession with fame is completely sick, and everything that has happened since the flood is just feeding into it... i seriously worry about his kids... have to wonder what he'll try next if this ploy for attention doesn't work out...
TROYVINNETTI *10 hours ago 4 likes 0 dislikes*

@TROYVINNETTI: exactly... he's like one of those parents who makes their kid sick so they can get sympathy... it's horrible...
BOBN4Apples *10 hours ago 5 likes 1 dislike*

lol funny video cant wait for frank nevis to give another interview so you guys can do this to that one hope this guy is this crazy 24/7
IMRICHBITCH *9 hours ago 13 likes 2 dislikes*

Thanks guys for all the views and likes check out our other videos on our channel click the link at the top of the page

AutoTuneYourMom *9 hours ago 120 likes 0 dislikes*

RE: Frank Nevis

Roper State University Online
Professor: Dr. David Henry
Class: Cultural & Media Studies - **CMS 102**
www.RoperStateUniversity.edu/forum/CMS/102
Page: 1 of 6

Dr. David Henry (dhenry@faculty.roperstate.edu) wrote:

RE: Frank Nevis. Your assignment for Monday is to watch Greg Morgan's interview with Frank Nevis (available here *www.youtube.com/user/wnn/greg morganinterviewsfranknevis?blend=1&ob=5#p/f/2/8c6tcrwwTto*) and then compose a 250-word reply discussing how Frank Nevis fits into the criteria outlined by Evans and Williamson in last night's reading. Your discussion may include response to your classmates' replies to this assignment.

Jeremy Tuchi (jtuchi@students.roperstate.edu) wrote:

I thought that it was really interesting the way that Frank Nevis talked about himself as though he was a product. People are not products, but sometimes we say that people are products, like the way a person can be a product of his environment. Frank Nevis is trying to create an environment in which he can be a product.

He wants to be famous so that he can become more famous. I thought it was really interesting the way that Greg Morgan tried to see if he felt any remorse for what he had done to the other people in Gill Falls and the way that he kept saying that it wasn't his fault. Frank Nevis is detached and emotionally numb, like Evans and Williamson talk about sometimes happens to famous people. It doesn't seem like he cares at all about the woman whose hand was hurt when she tried to stop the boat from going over the waterfall. It is really sad that Frank Nevis sees his children and especially his daughter Melissa as a way to get attention for himself. He doesn't even talk for a second about what the kids are going through - just glosses over it and goes right back to talking about himself. Then he tries to act like him being famous is all about his family - like he is doing it so that they can have a better life. He is delusional and self-centered, just like Evans and Williamson talk about famous people being.

Ginny Straub (gstraub@students.roperstate.edu) wrote:

The fallacy at the center of Frank Nevis's professed worldview - and resultant "plan" - is that celebrity is a transitive property: that "good" celebrity (what Evans and Williamson call the "public affirmation and celebration of talent, action, or personality") is indistinguishable in both quality and currency from "bad" celebrity (the "public scorn ascribed to those whose actions or personalities society has deemed unacceptable or out of accord with its professed tastes or morality, bestowed upon those whose actions / personalities are of such gross nature as to merit the dubious honor of social counterpoint"). The stupefying aspect of this interview is less Frank Nevis's relentless assertion of himself and more his tone deaf approach: he seems unaware that by these statements and actions he is making himself a veritable pariah: much more famous, but no more (and undoubtedly even less) bankable as any sort of public figure. One has to wonder, while watching this interview, if Frank Nevis would be oblivious to this contradiction had his obsession with fame not blinded him to it. Is he truly unbalanced / crazy / delusional, or has he merely become so mired in his own quest for celebrity that he has lost his, if not moral, then at least let us say logical compass? The question is pertinent, if only for the sake of his family: while it is true (as he says himself) that he never put any of his children in harm's way, one has to wonder how long he can be trusted to maintain this boundary if the fame he seeks continues to elude him.

John Davis (jdavis@students.roperstate.edu) wrote:

I think what happened to Frank Nevis is what can happen to anyone when they get too caught up in society's craziness and forget themselves. It is easy for anyone to get lost in the world - there are many distractions and many things that can make you forget yourself. Frank Nevis needs to get back to himself and stop worrying about what society cares about. This world is not forever only life with God is forever and Frank Nevis has forgotten that. I feel sorry for Frank. I feel sorry for his kids because Frank cannot love them. We cannot love unless we feel loved, and Frank is looking for society to love him. He doesn't know that the only endless and unconditional love is from

God. If I could talk to Frank, I would tell him to go to Church and get down on his knees and to talk to God. I bet if he talked to God he wouldn't do anymore craziness and we wouldn't hear any more about him. Evans and Williamson talk about how trying to be famous can make you crazy, and that's what it has done to Frank. They say that "for some people fame can become an obsession on the same level as any other form of obsession, be it positive (the "goal" obsession) or negative (the "fear" obsession)." This is what has happened to Frank: he is obsessed with his goal and fearful that he will not achieve it.

Mike Roehmer (mroehmer@students.roperstate.edu) wrote:

Frank Nevis wants to be famous, that is clear from his interview with World News Network's Greg Morgan. What is not clear is why he wants to be famous. He says that if you aren't famous then you are a nobody. Even when Greg Morgan replies that you can be somebody to your friends and family and not be famous, Frank Nevis disagrees and continues to say that you are a nobody if you are not famous. I wonder what happened to Frank Nevis to make him think that it was not good enough to be loved by your friends and family. Evans and Williamson talk about examples of famous people who had unhappy childhoods, and felt like their parents didn't love them or whose parents didn't pay any attention to them. I wonder if Frank Nevis had a similar experience? One thing is for certain, and that is that Frank Nevis does not see things the way other people see them. Does this make him wrong? Just because we don't understand Frank

Nevis doesn't make him bad or evil. Maybe if we knew more about how he was raised we would understand why he wants to be famous so badly and then we would feel sorry for him, rather than hate him. Evans and Williamson say that people who are obsessed with fame are often suffering from depression, and think that being famous will make them happy. Frank Nevis definitely thinks that being famous will make him happy - I wonder if he is depressed when the cameras are off?

The Top Ten

All right folks welcome back to the show, Cameron Diaz will be out here in just a moment but right now it's time for tonight's top ten list! I know, I know. What can I say? They love the list. All right tonight we're doing the top ten things Frank Nevis's kids hope they never hear him say. Number ten: "All right, everyone in the car, we're going to try out my new invention." Number nine: "Ok, which one of you wants to make the family famous?" Number eight: "Don't worry, I know what I'm doing." Number seven: "It's your turn to go stay with Grandma." Number six: "If you want to make an omelette you have to break some eggs." Number five: "Don't worry, my new invention is almost completely safe." Number four: "I need a test dummy for my new invention - never mind, you want to come help daddy?" Number three: "Hey, remember our garage?" Number two: "Hey, remember our car?" And the number one thing Frank Nevis's kids hope they never hear him say: "Hey, where's

Melissa?" Oh, yeah, thank you. What can I say? They love the top ten...

To Whom It May Concern:

To Whom It May Concern:

Frank Nevis, Victoria Nevis, nee Lagrange, Sandra Nevis, William ("Billy") Nevis, June Nevis, Thomas ("Tommy") Nevis, and Melissa Nevis, hereafter referred to as Nevis Family, are now represented by the public relations firm of Harold Brochet and Associates, LLC, and any and all communications pertaining to usage including but not limited to appearances, interviews, likenesses, media portrayals, etc. (hereafter referred to as "usage") shall be directed to the offices of Harold Brochet and Associates, LLC, attention Louis Young, licensed agent. Any and all usage without the expressed and written approval of Louis Young or the Nevis Family is hereby disallowed and shall be pursued under defamation laws in the jurisdiction of its origin.

Louis Young, Agent
Harold Brochet and Associates, LLC
LYoung@HaroldBrochetandAssoc.com
www.HaroldBrochetandAssoc.com

www.Frankophile.bloghost.com

www.Frankophile.bloghost.com

In Frank We Trust

Title: *For Now We See Through a Glass, Darkly*
By: *Molly Fischer*

Hi Guys (all 176 of you)!

So first off I want to thank each and every one of you for following my blog, and I want to encourage all of you, if you haven't already, to join the associated Facebook group, which you can find at www.Facebook.com /group/ Frankophile. (For anyone new to the site: the Facebook group is where I post links and breaking news, the blog is for people to comment on and discuss everything going on with the Nevis family.)

So it's been a busy week for the Nevises! On Monday night we all got to hear Frank Nevis tell in his own words just what was going on behind the scenes during the so-called "Gill Falls Girl" prank. In his LIVE interview with Greg Morgan, Frank discussed everything from his plans to get his reality show back on the air (fingers crossed!) to the media conglomerates running our country. (A complete transcript of the interview, typed up by *BlueAngel-Fire23*, can be found by clicking here... Thanks BlueAngel!) It was a powerhouse interview for Frank, and I encourage everyone to either read BlueAngel's transcript or check out one of the (uncut!) videos of the interview, available on YouTube.

Then on Thursday we received word that the Nevis camp was moving on the offensive: several news organizations (a list, with links, is available here) reported that the family had signed on with the PR firm Harold Brochet and Associates, LLC. (This is the company, some readers may remember, most recently responsible for litigating reclusive author H.J. Kitchner's mistress's memoir into obscurity). Harold Brochet and Associates is a massive powerhouse of a firm, and I'm sure they're already hard at work rebranding the Nevises for a public unveiling. With a little bit of luck (you never know, but my fingers are crossed) they'll see the same potential in Frank that we do...

Those are the two major pieces of news so far this week, but before I go I'd like to close this entry with a reply to some of the emails I've received (sorry I can't reply to all).

Roger Steel sent us an email that read:

Molly, has Frank Nevis seen your blog / facebook group, and if so, what does he think of it?

Thanks for the email, Roger. As far as we know Frank has not looked at the blog or the Facebook group, which is to say that we have not received any indication that he has. However, we like to think that one day he will be scrolling around the internet and come across us, and know that at least a few of us out here get what he's all about :)

Timothy Greer sent a message to the Frankophile Facebook group that read:

I am supposed to write a paper about Frank Nevis for a sociology class. I came across a mention of your group and blog in an article in the Daily Dispatch-Chronicle Online. I've looked all over both pages and I still don't get it. What is it that makes Frank Nevis a big deal? The whole thing seems stupid to me. It seems like everyone is just flogging a dead horse. If there is any way that you can explain it to me, I would really appreciate it.

Thanks for the FB message, Timothy, and I will try to reply to it the best that I can. I think one thing about the whole situation that makes it so remarkable is something you yourself commented on: that at the end of the day there isn't much to the story. A guy (Frank Nevis) faked an event, managed to keep everyone going for a few days, and then the truth came out. In that aspect, the story isn't very remarkable at all. What is remarkable is the skill - the panache, even - with which Frank Nevis turned an implausible and false account into a major media sensation. Is it true that Frank Nevis just wanted to be famous? Certainly. But it is also true, we here at Frankophile feel, that in his quest for fame he stumbled on an insight into the nature of the modern media, and through that, into an insight about our culture and ourselves. Does the accidental quality of this discovery make it any less profound? Certainly not: remember that many of the world's greatest discoveries - electricity, silly putty, America, etc. - were accidents along the way to where the explorer / inventor / discoverer thought he was going.

Anyway, I hope that clears up some of the confusion, Timothy. Right now I'm late for class, so I'll say so long for now.

- Molly

Tonight on Talk Nation

Tonight on Talk Nation Frank Nevis, Rene Batchelor, and Dr. David Sellers discuss the future of news. I'm Phil Tanner, sitting in this week for Richard Becker, who is out with the flu. We all hope you feel better soon, Rich. All right, let's get right to it. Rene Batchelor joining us via satellite, you are the New Media Consultant for Frick and Burton, which is a, uh, help me out here it's a manufacturing conglomerate?

That's right we have interests in several manufacturing firms based in the United States and Europe. We have shares in a number of different companies and controlling shares in a few major corporations.

I see so major, major international business.

Correct.

All right and joining us in the studio are Frank Nevis and Dr. David Sellers. Dr. Sellers, you are the professor of Media and Cultural Studies at Whitlock College...

That's right.

... and you recently published an article, let me see if I can find it here, ah right, published an article called *Consuming Reality: Feeding the Hungry Media Market* in Anvil Magazine.

That's correct.

That's an interesting title I wonder if you could give our audience just a brief overview of some of the points you make.

Uh, certainly, well the idea was actually brought about by the story of, uh, of your other guest here, and the... uh, can I call them antics? that went on during the flooding in Gill Falls, Missouri, and... uh, I don't want to tell your story for you Frank.

No, that's ok.

Anyway maybe that's not important, but anyway I'm sure your viewers are already familiar with the whole saga... The idea was that news and news reporting and the role that the news plays in our lives has changed significantly since I was a child, primarily with the advent of portable technology... um, I make the point in the article that as soon as the portable videocamera and then the portable satellite uplink truck became available that, uh, that news became a race to see who could report on an event first. There was serious competition between news syndicates in, uh, in a new way. Whereas before the competition was between anchor personalities and... uh, I guess you would say cosmetic things... There was some exclusivity and things like this, with one news station having content that the other... that the other wouldn't have but there... there wasn't this kind of frantic scurrying like you see now.

I see and one of the points I found so interesting in your article was that you, uh, you point out how in this race to cover a story before the story has had time to, to, uh, develop I guess is what I'm trying to say, before all the facts are in or are available to the newsperson on the scene, that there is a serious push now to get a story on the air or out onto the web as quickly as possible, and that, uh, that this is the way that news agencies scoop each other these days.

That's right the point I was making or, uh, trying to make at least was that the people who suffer for this are the viewers, because they are often given, if not incorrect information then let's say incomplete information... Uh, and the idea is that this is the antithesis of news reporting, because the news is supposed to give people *more* information, not, you know, not confuse them.

I see and this seems like a good time to introduce our third guest this evening, although I'm sure he needs no introduction at this point... Frank Nevis is the man responsible for the so-called "Gill Falls Girl" prank or hoax or fraud, depending on who you talk to... Uh, Frank, people, well some people at least, are making you out to be the sort of unofficial poster child for the flaws in the modern media... What do you say to people who call you... how did one commentator put it.... ah, here it is: "harbinger of the coming New Media apocalypse?"

Well I, huh, I didn't read that, uh, that particular piece.

Well, I mean, still, you've heard people say things like this.

Uh, well, like I said I haven't heard it put quite that way but... uh, you know I think it's interesting that people see some kind of... some kind of larger, uh, social, uh... thing going on with what... uh, with what happened with us, you know with my family... I don't... uh, I don't know that it's... that it's you know something that... something that you can make all that... something that has that much, uh... significance.

Still, I mean, you can't deny, I mean you're not un-aware of the fact, or you certainly weren't unaware of the fact that you could only have done what you did in the way that you did it with the advent of things like cell phone cameras and YouTube... Within hours of the story going out there was a video on YouTube that you shot with your cell phone camera of you searching or I guess pretending to search for your daughter, I mean... I think the thing that people are so, I guess impressed would be the only word for it, impressed by is the savvy with which you pulled the whole thing off. You can't tell us that it was just dumb luck.

No, I mean, I... It wasn't dumb luck I guess I just didn't... Uh, I didn't see it as anything particularly special or you know strategically brilliant... It just seemed like the right thing to do for what I was trying to do at the time.

And I think this goes right back to your point Dr. Sellers, that with a little bit of savvy a person could string the whole country along, for a little while at least.

Yes, that's, uh, that's sort of the point I was making in my Anvil Magazine piece, that it does take a little bit of savvy, but not nearly as much savvy as you would hope. I mean you would hope it would take some doing to pull the wool over everyone's eyes, but the problem with the media landscape these days is that it just doesn't.

All right. Ms. Batchelor, your company, the company you work for and represent Frick and Burton has been accused of intentionally releasing misleading information to news agencies to try to assuage bad press from everything from human rights misconduct at some of the manufacturing plants in the South Pacific to, uh, to environmental protection code violations... What insight do you have to add to Mr. excuse me Dr. Sellers' point, that the new media is easily misled?

Well... I... I'm not sure I understand the question. You're asking me what sort of insight I have into... No, I don't think I understand the question.

I just mean that at a firm as large as Frick...

So you're asking me what sort of insight I can offer into... What? I don't think I have anything to offer. My job is to put the company's best face forward, to make sure that the public is aware of the innovations we have spearheaded in everything from manufacturing protocol to workplace safety... to, uh, uh, make sure that people are aware of the goods and services we offer... My job is to facilitate the public relations efforts of all of our subsidiaries so that we can...

I see so you're not...

No, not, uh... I'm getting the sense that you think that I'm some sort of master of propaganda, and that's not what I am at all, not what my job is at all.

I see why don't you tell us then just briefly what your job is.

My job is, uh, well it's like I said I facilitate and coordinate the public relations for all of our subsidiaries, so that includes co-branding, it includes advertising, it includes press announcements... I like to say that I'm not the public face of Frick and Burton, but I am the face behind the face.

Thank you that's quite an image. Frank Nevis I wonder if we could return to you for just a moment. Last Monday you did an interview with Greg Morgan, and then a few days later you signed on with the PR firm Harold Brochet and Associates. Were you not happy with how you came off in the interview?

Um... No, I wasn't... I wasn't unhappy... I mean unhappy isn't the right word. I didn't realize... I don't think I had a clear sort of idea of what, uh, of what was going to be, what people were going to.... I mean a clear idea of sort of how the game works, how this whole thing works so I wasn't unhappy, I just really felt like if I had gone in there with a little bit of a clearer idea of... Not of what I wanted to say but of how I wanted to say it I could have been a lot more, uh, I guess effective is the word, in conveying what I wanted to convey. So that's why we signed on with Harold Brochet... Uh, the idea is that they're just going to be, our guy Lou is going to be sort of our strategic commander through these next few months.

Your strategic commander?

Yeah, he's going to, you know, set up interviews and stuff like that so that people can hear what I have to say, and I'll have a chance to say it in the way that, uh, that it can best be, you know, heard and understood.

I see and I take it that this is one of those interviews?

... Uh, that was the idea yes.

All right, and how do you think it's going?

Uh, I don't know, well?

Phil, I'm sorry to break in here, but I really don't see what any of this has to do with Frick and Burton.

Uh, well...

Look I'm really... I apologize, but I'm going to, uh, I'm going to take this mic off and I'm going to go. Thank you for having me.

Ms. Batchelor it's, uh... Ms. Bachelor? Is she gone? All right we've lost Ms. Batchelor, Rene Batchelor, Head of Public Relations for Frick and Burton, joining us by satellite, and hopefully she will be able to join us again sometime in the near future.

Frank, can I ask you a question myself, while Phil is getting this sorted out?

Certainly.

What sort of education do you have in this field? I mean have you studied communications or media or anything like that?

Uh, no... I mean not formally, but I... You know I've always loved science and technology, as you can probably guess... We were the first family on our street... Actually I think we might have been the first family in Gill Falls to have a home computer and we were the first household that got online, you know, back in '94 or '95, whenever that was and so... uh, you know and so as the technology has changed we've more or less tried to keep pace with it so it's, uh, it's just something I've always been interested in. I know that people are... Some people think it's really, I don't know, clever or something what I did and I guess it kind of is but it also, it's also just pretty obvious that you can do what I did if you, you know, if you look at the thing for long enough.

Amazing.

Dr. Sellers, what do you make of everything Frank just said?

I was just saying that it was amazing that someone without any formal education in this field could, uh, I guess do what Frank did. Would you be interested, Frank, in coming and talking to my New Media class? I think it could be a very informative experience for my students.

Uh, I'd love to, let me just, uh, let me just clear it with Lou and we'll, I guess we'll be in touch. Does that work?

Certainly. Thank you, I think it would be just terrific.

All right I can see that we're losing the, uh, losing the thread a little bit so, uh, let me just ask you both in closing what's next on the agenda?

Well Lou has us set up to meet with some people from a couple of different networks to try and get the wheels turning on the show again, and then I guess we're going to have to go look for someplace to live after that, because our place is a total loss. On the other hand, I think we're all enjoying the hotel life. The kids have eaten more room service macaroni and cheese...

Terrific and Dr. Sellers, what's next for you?

Well I've been approached by Victor and Straub...

The publishing house?

...uh, that's right, the publishing house Victor and Straub and we're talking about expanding the *Consuming Media* piece, uh, they want me to expand the *Consuming Media* piece into a book.

Well best of luck with that and you'll have to come back on and tell us all about it when that book comes out.

That would be wonderful, it would be my pleasure.

Well that's it for us, be sure to tune in tomorrow night when Richard Becker will hopefully be back and will talk to Cameron Diaz about her new movie. Until then I'm Phil Tanner saying, good night.

*www.watchout.com/forum/franknevis/topic/whydoesan
yonestillcareaboutfranknevis?*

Topic: Why does anyone still care about Frank Nevis?
posted by: RobRider28 *40 minutes ago*

Can somebody PLEASE help me out here? I have no
idea why on earth people still care about this guy.
Hasn't the timer on his fifteen minutes sounded
yet?!?! I get that we're all feeling embarrassed that he
snowed us the way he did, but that doesn't mean we
need to go around saying he's some sort of new media
genius. He's NOT. He got us, fair and square, but now
it's OVER. Let's please move on.

Reply 1
posted by: GeeGeePeterson *38 minutes ago*

For as obnoxious as this is getting, I have to sort of
admire the guy... Yes he is a totally unscrupulous and
slimy individual, but he is milking this thing for all
it's worth... He is the epitome of "there is no such
thing as bad publicity" thinking...

Reply 2
posted by: BrianThatcher *35 minutes ago*

Whenever a celebrity dies of a drug overdose all of
the other celebrities talk about their own past addictions for the next month when they're on talk shows...
Whenever a disaster happens a bunch of celebrities

get on tv to pitch a charity... Maybe we shake our heads, but we don't get outraged when an already famous person tries to make themselves more famous by attaching their name to something everyone is talking about... Shameless self-promotion is nothing new... Celebrities have been doing it with calculated crassness since the invention of media... Frank Nevis was smart enough to do the same thing when the tools became available to him... My hat is off to him.

Reply 3
posted by: RitaFalco90 *30 minutes ago*

Brian: the difference between Frank Nevis and the celebrities you mention is that those celebrities are already famous - they are famous for doing something that made them famous, i.e. they are actors or musicians who the public has elevated to a position of fame in response to their talent. They aren't just famous for being famous or for trying to be famous. Frank Nevis has nothing to offer, he just wants attention.

Reply 4
posted by: Tom Jilette *24 minutes ago*

Rita: celebrities aren't famous just for wanting to be famous? Really? What about all of those people on shows like *The Bachelor* and *Big Brother?* What about the Kardashians? What do you call Paris Hilton?

Reply 5
posted by: Anonymous *23 minutes ago*

Frank Nevis is a student of celebrity and pop culture. His work shows us something about ourselves. His life is performance art.

Reply 6
posted by: RitaFalco90 *19 minutes ago*

Tom: I see your point. Anonymous: It's hard to take something seriously when its author won't admit to having written it.

Reply 7
posted by: TrishRich76 *8 minutes ago*

I agree with anonymous. Love him or hate him, he's certainly onto something.

WATCH OUT! is a community discussion forum. It is our belief that much of the world's news is kept from U.S. audiences, and that to know what is really going on in the world we must look beyond the (domestically-based) so-called "World News" networks. This is a place for the free exchange of information and ideas.

Not a member yet? Register by clicking here.

The Nevis Family Speaks - Part 3

Title: **The Nevis Family Speaks - Part 3**
Uploaded by: FrankNevis *1 hour ago*
Duration: 5:13

Description: You may think you know Frank Nevis, but frankly you don't know Frank. *Directed by Akiro Hitchiyaro. Edited by Gwen Lewis. Produced by Harold Brochet and Associates, LLC.*

Opening: White background with black text superimposed: *"You may think you know Frank Nevis."*

Fade in on montage of clips from news coverage of the Gill Falls flood, the search for Melissa Nevis, YouTube videos uploaded by Frank Nevis, and subsequent television interviews.

Fade out to white with black text superimposed: *"But Frankly, you don't know Frank."*

Fade in on footage of Frank and Victoria playing with their children in a park, pushing them on the swings, spinning them on the merry-go-round, etc. Footage of Frank and Victoria holding hands, hugging, kissing. Footage of Frank and Victoria reading to the kids as they are put to bed.

Frank Nevis (voiceover): I think I'm just like anybody else. I love my family. I would do anything for my family.

Smash cut to Greg Morgan interview: Greg Morgan: *What do you have to say for yourself?... I find it completely fantastic that your neighbors aren't ready to drive you out of town on a rail. I mean that's a fantastic notion to me... People are reviling you. They're saying your children should be taken away from you...*

Cut to shot of Frank Nevis, sitting on park bench.

Frank Nevis: Hello everyone. By now a lot of you know my face. You also know what I did, and what I said about it later. I know that those things made a lot of you angry. I'm not going to sit here and rationalize or explain what I've done or why I did it. If you've seen and heard my interviews, then you've already heard the best explanation I can give. What I'm here to do now is apologize to the thousands of you who felt misled by my words and actions. I am truly and deeply sorry. I've been called everything from self-centered to crazy, and to the people who said those things I say: you're right. You're one-hundred percent correct: what I did was self-centered, and it was crazy, and it was foolish. I put good people at risk - good people whose only thought was to help my family. To them I say again: I am sorry.

I also want to apologize to the hundreds, if not thousands, of you who, after hearing my story, sent money to the various charities working to repair the flood damage in Gill Falls. I want to assure you that those charities had no notion of my actions, and that your donation has been used only for the recovery efforts in the town of Gill Falls. If you have any lingering hesitation, you should know that I have asked those charities, as well as the Gill Falls Chamber of Commerce, to exclude our home and our property from their clean-up efforts, and direct any volunteers to expend their energies elsewhere, where their help is greatly needed. None of your donation money is going to help me or my family in any way. I regret that the real tragedy in Gill Falls has been overshadowed by my fabrication, and I want to remind everyone that the need in Gill Falls is still very great, and every effort and donation has been and is greatly appreciated by the good people there, who are just trying to get their lives back to normal.

I hope that one day soon we will be able to put all of this behind us. Thanks for watching.

Cut to shot of the Nevis family, holding hands, leaving the park, walking into the sunset. Fade out to white with superimposed black text: *"For more please visit www. FrankNevis.com."*

Frank Nevis's Online Act of Contrition

www.Frankophile.bloghost.com
In Frank We Trust

Title: *Frank Nevis's Online Act of Contrition*
By: *Molly Fischer*

Hello Everybody!
I'm going to be late for my next class, but I had to sit down and dash off a quick post because FRANK NEVIS HAS JUST RELEASED A NEW VIDEO ON HIS YOU-TUBE CHANNEL! (follow the link to watch: *http://www.youtube.com/franknevis/thenevisfamilyspeakspart3/watch?v=I9tWZB7OUSU&feature=related*)
Right off the bat, you're going to notice that this five-minute video (his longest yet) produced by Harold Brochet and Associates (the Nevis family's hired PR firm) is the most professional-looking of Frank's videos (makes me wonder what they're paying HB&A, lol) - mainly because it's NOT one of Frank's videos: it is directed by Akiro Hitchiyaro, who (a quick Google search reveals) has worked mostly on Japanese commercials. But this isn't a bad thing, but I did find myself missing the candid charm of the self-portrait videos that preceded this one (TNFS Parts 1 and 2). The professional packaging, however, may do wonders to get this video seen and passed around the web, which is (of course) the goal, but more so with this vid because this is an APOLOGY (shock and awe).
All right, so not shock and awe. You saw it coming, didn't you? There's only one course outlined in the PR playbook for this situation: 1) once you attract an audience by making them hate you and object to you, then you

2) win them over with contrition, so you can 3) keep them with affection. The casual viewer may see this video as the tolling bell marking the end of the Nevis chapter - an apology before we all move on - but what we are seeing may in fact be Frank's savviest move to date. He apologizes to everyone: those who donated money, those who volunteered in Gill Falls, and to the general public, those with no direct beef but who feel generally annoyed / upset / outraged by his actions. He OWNS UP to his misconduct (confession), even stating that he has told charities and the people in charge of cleanup in Gill Falls to FORGO WORKING ON HIS HOUSE OR PROPERTY (sacrifice / contrition / punishment), and expresses his hope that "one day soon we will be able to put all of this behind us." He even thanks us for watching.

This new video is a brilliant move, and it should be, with a PR firm now calling the shots. Even still, the real centerpiece of this video is Frank: his earnest delivery and heartfelt tone make it almost impossible to not believe every word he's saying.

Cripes, I am so late. Gotta run. You don't need my input anyway... watch the vid and post your comments. TTYL - Molly

www.FrankNevis.com

HOME

[Page not displaying correctly? Get the latest version of Flash by clicking here.]

Welcome to FrankNevis.com, your online source for straight-from-the-horse's mouth information about Frank Nevis and the Nevis Family. This site is currently under construction, so check back soon as more content is being added daily.

Copyright © Frank Nevis / Contact the webmaster by clicking here / Site maintained by Internet Technology Solutions LLC, a subsidiary of Harold Brochet and Associates, LLC.

ABOUT FRANK & THE FAM

Frank was born in Mellor, Missouri to Graham and Cynthia Nevis. Even from an early age, Frank's twin passions were performance and invention. He would often sit his parents down on the couch in the living room of the family's modest ranch-style home and then grandly reveal his latest creation - a shopping cart with various compartments (so the bread and eggs wouldn't get crushed), a bicycle with padded pedals (so a slip wouldn't result in bruised shins), an alarm clock housing with a special lever that made hitting the snooze button faster and easier, just to name a few - which had been standing before them, shrouded in mystery and covered by Frank's rocket ship bedsheets.

Frank's passion for science and the performing arts stayed with him through his time at Mellor High School, where he worked on or performed in nearly every theatrical production the school put on during his time and, his junior year, where he won first prize in the school's annual science fair.

After high school Frank attended the University of Missouri. It was here that he met Victoria Lagrange. Victoria was a star athlete, competing for the school's Track and Field team and, though she did not share Frank's scientific or theatrical ambitions, she more than matched him in enthusiasm: Frank has often said that he had never met anyone who approached life with the same aggressive passion as himself until he met Victoria. It was love at first sight, and in the summer following their junior year, Frank and Victoria were married.

Following graduation Frank applied and interviewed for jobs with NASA and several private companies. However, despite his many years of private study, these companies did not feel that Frank would be of use to them - not without a postgraduate degree, at least. The frustration Frank felt - at being judged on his "resume self" and not on his merits or demonstrable abilities - only fueled Frank's fire and, one year after finishing his undergraduate degree, Frank returned to the University of Missouri to pursue his master's degree.

A higher degree was not in the cards for Frank, however, as during his first semester back at school Victoria became pregnant with their first child, Sandra. Frank left school and the family moved to Gill Falls to be closer to Victoria's mother (Frank's parents had since retired and moved out of state). There Frank worked during the day and continued to work on his own inventions at night in the family's small garage. His tireless efforts eventually earned him two patents from the United States Patent Office.

Today Frank and Victoria's enthusiasm is stronger than ever. "You only get one life," says Victoria. "You're only in this world for a little while, so I say you have to go out there and get busy getting after whatever it is you want to do." It is a sentiment that Frank echoes. "Anybody can have a great life," he says, "but it takes hard work and it takes not giving up. That's what we tell our kids. Their lives can be whatever they decide to make them."

INVENTIONS

Patents - click on the invention for more information

US Patent No. 6705687 Oscillating Blender
Oscillating blender. Patent No. 6705687. Issued to: **Frank Nevis**. Filed: October 16, 2001. PCT Filed: February 13, 2001 ...
http://www.uspto.gov/670567

US Patent No. 6995749 Accordion Closet Organizer
Accordion closet organizer. Patent No. 6995749. Issued to: **Frank Nevis**. Filed: May 23, 2003. PCT Filed: September 24, 2003 ...
http://www.uspto.gov/6995749

Patents Pending - click on the invention for more information

The Collapsible Shoe Tree
Do you carry a lot of shoes when you travel? Then the collapsible shoe tree is the invention you've been waiting for! With its hinged arms and removable base the collapsible shoe tree breaks down small, but stands up tall

when needed! Patent filed with the United States Patent and Trademark Office, filing number 9230723.

The World's Best Toothpaste Dispenser

Maybe you've seen other toothpaste dispensers in the past, but this one blows them all out of the water! If you have kids, you know what a mess toothbrushing can become. Eliminate one source of disaster with Frank's easy-to-use pump-action toothpaste dispenser. Unlike other toothpaste dispensers, which rely on a gravity feed and can leak, Frank's toothpaste dispenser is powered by a pressurized bladder which expands from the bottom of the chamber up, giving you an even flow of toothpaste and making sure that none gets left in the bottom of the tube. Easy, and economical. Patent filed with the United States Patent and Trademark Office, filing number 10293932.

The Double-Ended Screwdriver

Tired of always searching for the "other" screwdriver? Does it feel like every screw head takes a phillips, and all you've got is a flathead (or vice versa)? Then you'll love Frank's Double-Ended Screwdriver. Both ends of a single piece of tempered steel are fashioned into the two common screw styles. The rubberized, ergonomically-designed handle slides freely from one end to the other until the pin is engaged, locking it in place. Switch from phillips to flathead in back in the blink of an eye! Patent filed with the United States Patent and Trademark Office, filing number 11203923.

Other Inventions - click on the invention for more information

The Bib Shirt

If your kids are anything like Frank and Victoria Nevis's kids, then you know what a mess they can make at meal time, especially of themselves. Cut down on your cleaning time with the bib shirt. These shirts, available in four colors and styles, have a panel of bib material sewn into the front, right in the "splash zone." Perfect for that messy eater in your family.

Kitty Comb Cuffs

Love your cat, but hate having cat hair on your ankles from when kitty wants some attention? Then these easy-to-put-on cuffs will have you (and your cat) purring with pleasure! Twelve inches tall and secured with a velcro strip, these gaiters have a micro-fine "comb-like" surface that will gently comb through your kitty's hair as she rubs against it. Collects kitty's shedding hair for easy disposal, and leaves your pants and ankles hair-free!

KIDS' SPACE

Sandra

Sandra is 11 years old. She likes going to school and playing with her friends. Her favorite foods are pizza and butter pecan ice cream. When she grows up she wants to be either a postal worker or a teacher. Her favorite subjects in school are math and reading.

Billy

Billy is 10 years old. Like his mother, Billy's first love is sports. He plays baseball, football, and soccer. He wants to be a professional athlete when he grows up. His favorite foods are tacos and hamburgers. Billy also loves comic books and going to the movies.

June

June is 8 years old. She loves going to school, and she especially likes riding the bus. Her favorite foods are corn on the cob and macaroni and cheese. When June grows up she wants to design clothes.

Tommy

Tommy is 7 years old. Tommy wants to be an inventor, like his father. Tommy likes helping his father in the garage. He also likes boats and going fast on his bicycle. When he grows up, Tommy wants to be either a ship's captain or race motorcycles.

Melissa

Melissa is 6 years old. Melissa likes going to kindergarten and likes her teacher, Ms. Lewis. Melissa's favorite foods are whipped cream and pancakes. Melissa likes swimming and going to the beach. She also loves the zoo. When Melissa grows up, she wants to work at the zoo, especially with the elephants.

tions LLC, a subsidiary of Harold Brochet and Associates, LLC.

STORE

Did you see an invention you liked on the "Inventions" page? Many of Frank's inventions are available for sale at the FrankNevis.com Store. The Store is also the place to find Nevis family tee-shirts, postcards, stickers, and so much more! Come in and browse around, we're sure you'll find something you like.

Copyright © Frank Nevis / Contact the webmaster by clicking <u>here</u> / Site maintained by Internet Technology Solutions LLC, a subsidiary of Harold Brochet and Associates, LLC.

MAILING LIST

Want to be the first to know whenever there's big (or small) news from the Nevis family? Then sign up for our mailing list! The FrankNevis.com mailing list is the place to be to get all of the latest from the Nevis family. Sign up by clicking <u>here</u>.

SOUNDING BOARD

Do you have something to say to Frank, Victoria, or the kids? You can send an email to <u>contact@frank nevis.com</u>. Frank and Victoria read all of the emails they receive, and try to reply to as many personally as they can. You can also connect with the Nevis Family on Facebook by clicking <u>here</u>.

THE NEVIS FAMILY IN THE NEWS

Frank talks to Phil Tanner of Talk Nation. Click the link below to watch a clip and read commentary. *www.NationalNewsNetwork.com/programs/talknation/ep293/clip1*

Frank talks to Greg Morgan. Click the link to watch the full interview. *www.youtube.com/user/wnn/gregmorganinterviewsgranknevis?blend=1&ob=5#p/f/2/8c6tcrwwTto*

PopCultureWatch

Hello and welcome to PopCultureWatch, the only place on your TV for all the latest celebrity news. I'm Brad Hanner, and tonight the name at the top of the marquee is Frank Nevis. Since signing on with well-known PR firm Harold Brochet and Associates the Nevis Family has been firing on all cylinders, full speed ahead with both barrels blazing. Earlier this week we saw Frank riding a chair on the popular news-and-talk show Talk Nation. The topic was the future of news, and Frank had this to say:

"I think it's interesting that people see some kind of... some kind of larger, uh, social, uh... thing going on with what... uh, with what happened with us, you know with my family... I don't... uh, I don't know that it's... that it's you know something that... something that you can make all that... something that has that much, uh... significance."

Eloquently put, Frank. This appearance was quickly followed by a new YouTube video depicting the Nevis Family playing together in a park, and a 3-minute speech from Frank in which he apologizes to any and everyone his actions may have hurt. Now this video was uploaded by the user FrankNevis in name only: this video and, we can assume, any more that appear in the near future, was and will be the product and property of Harold Brochet and Associates, LLC. And last but not least, this week saw the launch of FrankNevis.com, another Harold Brochet and Associates production featuring everything from a catalog of the Nevis kids' favorite foods to a shop selling souvenir "Gill Falls Girl" tee-shirts. You heard it here first, folks. Truth is officially stranger than fiction.

The Nevis Family Newsletter #1

From: donotreply@franknevis.com
To: mailinglist@franknevis.com
Subject: The Nevis Family Newsletter #1

Hello everyone, and thanks for joining the mailing list! This mailing list is the best way to stay informed about all of the exciting things going on with the Nevis Family. (Please note that the email address from which this email was sent does not accept incoming email; if you wish to reply to something in the newsletter please do so through the "Sounding Board" page at FrankNevis.com.)

We have an awful lot of news to pack into this first newsletter! First of all, some of you will be interested to know that Melissa has lost her first tooth! The Tooth Fairy visited and Melissa is now the proud owner of a crisp dollar bill, which she has not let out of her sight since the moment it appeared under her pillow (the other kids are mighty jealous!).

In other family news, the end of the school year is coming up fast, and the kids couldn't be more excited. As some of you may know, our kids have been out of school since the flooding back in Gill Falls. For the other children back home, the flood meant almost no break at all from their studies, as the Chamber of Commerce quickly organized temporary classrooms in some multi-purpose facilities that weren't as badly damaged by the flooding. However, we've been on the road so much with everything that's been going on that the kids ended up with a nice long break - far too long, if you ask Frank and me! After we got a little more settled we were able to enroll the kids in school here (we're staying with my mother in Headon, for the moment), and between being the new kids in school and everything else, the transition has been a rough one. Summer can't come soon enough! Louis (our agent from Harold Brochet) is setting up some meetings for Frank in Hollywood, and so we're trying to work it out so that when the school year ends we'll be able to take the kids to Disneyland (yay!).

Which leads me right into the next bit of news: Frank is meeting with some television people to talk about getting the show back on its feet and on the air! With all of the new interest in our family and in Frank's inventions Louis feels that our prospects are very good, and says that several conversations he's had have been "very promising"! That means everybody out there, keep your fingers crossed!

The website is up and looks FANTASTIC! We are so excited to finally have a site where people can see what Frank has been working on. We've been talking about it for years, but something else always came up before we could get around to doing it. A BIG "thank you" to the web design folks at Harold Brochet and Associates! One thing to note: there is another website selling "Gill Falls Girl" tee-shirts... THIS WEBSITE IS NOT ASSOCIATED WITH US. We have sent several letters to them asking them to take their website down, but so far they have not complied. Until they do, please tell your friends and family that the only place for OFFICIAL Gill Falls Girl and Nevis Family merchandise is WWW.FRANKNEVIS.COM/STORE.HTML

In more unpleasant news (boo!), we are heading to court this week so that a judge can rule on whether the Search and Rescue team that looked for the boat after it went over the falls has any right to legal recourse against us. Our lawyer, David, says that we can make a strong case for not being liable, but still it's keeping me up at night. If the judge says that they have a case then it opens the door for pretty much everybody else. I'm very conflicted emotionally about this as well, because on one hand I see their point. Even still, I don't think these are the measures that neighbors are supposed to go to against one another. When Frank and I moved to Gill Falls, one of the reasons we liked it was that we saw Gill Falls as a small town where people knew their neighbors, and handled things among themselves. Oh, well. Anyway, please keep your fingers crossed for us.

Oh, and one last thing before I sign off: last night I was in the kitchen at mom's house when Frank came in from the garage holding something covered with a cloth. This is how he always comes in when he's made something new, and it's always very exciting. But this time, when I pulled the cloth away, there was a little black jewelry box with the most beautiful gold bracelet! It really lifted my spirits. It's so frustrating sometimes, now that everyone is talking about Frank like they know him, when really there is so much about him - like how sweet he is - that they just have no idea about. It makes me want to get up on the roof and start telling people at the top of my lungs. Oh, well. With a little bit of luck the show will get picked up and people will be able to see for themselves.

Thank you all for your ongoing love and support. Lots of love to everyone out there from all of us here.

Vicki & the Fam.

Rock for Relief

www.GorgonRecordsInc.com/NEWSANDEVENTS.html

Jefferson City, MO. - Gorgon Records, Inc., in association with Fallen Vodka and Pound of Flesh Promotions, is pleased to announce **Rock for Relief**, a one-day, five-band summer music festival to benefit the victims of flooding in Missouri.

Wrath, whose new single "Father Don't Make Me" takes its inspiration from the story of Melissa Nevis, a resident of Gill Falls, Missouri whose father told authorities that she had been carried away by the floodwaters, will headline.

Also on the bill is alt-rock trio **The Battling Nancies**, whose drummer Yves Mendes was born and raised in the Missouri capital of Jefferson City.

"We're all Missourians," Mendes says. "When something happens to one of us, it happens to all of us. When one of us needs help, we all pitch in to help. That's just how people are in Missouri."

Other acts on the bill include **Touchstone**, **The DeadEye Dolls**, and **The Bastille**. Tickets are $45.95 and are available here, or from your local ticketing agent.

The Facebook page Frank Nevis and the Nevis Family

Frank Nevis created the Facebook page **Frank Nevis and the Nevis Family**. *7 days ago*

Frank Nevis uploaded a profile picture for the Facebook page **Frank Nevis and the Nevis Family**. *7 days ago*

Frank Nevis updated the About section of the Info for the Facebook page **Frank Nevis and the Nevis Family**. Frank Nevis wrote: "The Nevis Family is Frank and Victoria and their children Sandra, Billy, June, Tommy, and Melissa." *7 days ago*

Frank Nevis updated the website information for the Facebook page **Frank Nevis and the Nevis Family**. Frank Nevis updated the website to: "www.FrankNevis. com, twitter.com/FrankNevis" *7 days ago*

Frank Nevis updated the contact information for the Facebook page **Frank Nevis and the Nevis Family**.

Frank Nevis updated the email contact to: "FrankNevis @FrankNevis.com" *7 days ago*

Frank Nevis updated the Administrator list for the Facebook page **Frank Nevis and the Nevis Family**. Frank Nevis added Victoria Nevis to the Administrator list. *7 days ago*

Frank Nevis wrote on the wall for the Facebook page **Frank Nevis and the Nevis Family**: Hello everyone! This is the OFFICIAL Facebook page for Me, Victoria, and the kids. "Like" us, leave a comment on our wall, and check back as we will be posting all the latest family news! *7 days ago*

Frank Nevis created the photo album "Weekend in L.A." for the Facebook page **Frank Nevis and the Nevis Family**. *6 days ago*

Frank Nevis added 6 new pictures to the photo album "Weekend in L.A." *6 days ago*

Frank Nevis commented on his photo in the album "Weekend in L.A.": "Ticket in hand, headed to La-La-Land..." *6 days ago*

Frank Nevis commented on his photo in the album "Weekend in L.A.": "In front of the Chinese Theatre..." *6 days ago*

Frank Nevis commented on his photo in the album "Weekend in L.A.": "Under the Hollywood sign... Can't wait to come back here with the fam!" *6 days ago*

Frank Nevis commented on his photo in the album "Weekend in L.A.": "Waiting for my makeup before going on "Talk Nation"... do I look nervous?" *6 days ago*

Frank Nevis commented on his photo in the album "Weekend in L.A.": "On the Walk of Fame..." *6 days ago*

Frank Nevis commented on his photo in the album "Weekend in L.A.": "At the airport, getting ready to fly home... Excited to see the fam, but will be glad to get back to the coast... What can I say? I love L.A.!" *6 days ago*

Frank Nevis posted a link on the wall for the Facebook page **Frank Nevis and the Nevis Family**: www. FrankNevis.com/STORE.html *5 days ago*

Frank Nevis commented on his post: The FrankNevis.com Store is the only place to find OFFICIALLY LICENSED Nevis Family merchandise... ACCEPT NO IMITATIONS! *5 days ago.*

Rock for Relief: Just Announced

www.GorgonRecordsInc.com/NEWSANDEVENTS.html

Jefferson City, MO. - Just announced: the **Rock for Relief** summer music festival will feature a **special surprise guest**! We can't tell you who it is, but rest assured that this will be an appearance you won't want to miss! **Wrath**, **The Battling Nancies**, **Touchstone**, **The Dead-Eye Dolls**, **The Bastille** and now **a special surprise guest**! Tickets are $45.95 and are available <u>here</u>, or from your local ticketing agent.

Judge Rules in Favor of NMSARC

Judge Rules in Favor of NMSARC
by Phil Rebbing, court reporter
www.JeffersonCityTribune.com/news/courtnotices/923320

Jefferson City, MO - Frank Nevis may be looking to a brighter future, but the memory of the events that transpired two months ago in Gill Falls aren't fading so easily - at least not for the rescue workers who were on the front lines of the search for Frank's allegedly missing daughter, Melissa. Today Judge Randolph Brighton ruled in favor of the Northern Missouri Search and Rescue Coalition, stating that Frank and Victoria Nevis are responsible for the expense of the rescue operation, undertaken as a result of the hoax they perpetrated.

"We just want what's right," said Drew Brown, a representative from NMSARC, who was present during the court proceedings. "We don't think it's right that the taxpayers should have to foot the bill for Frank and Victoria's prank."

The Nevis's lawyer David Green, however, disagrees.

"We plan to appeal the decision," he said. "There is no legal precedent for this sort of thing in the state of Missouri. We count Search and Rescue under municipally-provided services. If this decision is allowed to stand, where will it end?"

The ruling, as it stands, sets a precedent for anyone who feels that they have suffered monetarily or otherwise as a result of the Nevises' actions to seek recompense. The estimated cost for the Search and Rescue operation stands at $35,000.

Phil Rebbing is a regular contributor to the Jefferson City Tribune. Contact him directly at PhilRebbing@Jefferson CityTribune.com. A subscription to the print version of this newspaper is available at www.JeffersonCityTribune .com/print/subscriptions

About *@FrankNevis*

239 Tweets / 83 Following / 1,912 Followers / 230 Listed

Bio: Frank Nevis is a father, inventor, and TV personality. Find out more about him at www.FrankNevis.com

@FrankNevis
> Leaving the courthouse now... David says not to worry... Filing appeal on Monday *10 hours ago*

@FrankNevis
> Melissa feeling a little bit sick... taking her to the doc to make sure nothing serious *6 hours ago*

@FrankNevis
> Doc says just indigestion, Melissa is fine... Vicki is upset about judges decision *4 hours ago*

@FrankNevis
> Just talked to Louis... he set up a meeting with some people from NTC, heading back out to LA on Tuesday, going to take the fam... *3 hours ago*

@FrankNevis
> Just told kids we're taking them to LA and we promised them disneyland... we've got some very excited children on our hands! *3 hours ago*

@FrankNevis
> Applebees for dinner... Melissa wants buffalo wings... guess her stomach feels better! A marga-

rita for mom is probably in the cards... *2 hours ago*

@*FrankNevis*
Bedtime for the kids means I get to do some tinkering in the garage :)... hope Barb doesnt mind *30 minutes ago*

Molly Fischer shared a link

Molly Fisher shared a link on the wall for the Facebook Group **Frankophile**: www.frankophile.bloghost.com/solongfarewell *10 minutes ago*

Molly Fisher commented on her link: Hey guys check out my my latest blog post. *10 minutes ago*

So long, farewell

www.Frankophile.bloghost.com
In Frank We Trust

Title: *So Long, Farewell*
By: *Molly Fischer*

Hello all you Frankophiles (all 451 of you)!
So I've been anticipating this post for a while, but I didn't think it would be this hard to write. I've been sitting here, staring at the little blinking cursor, for almost an hour, just trying to think of how to start. They say it's best

to go back to the beginning and tell the truth, so that's what I'm going to do.

As some of you may know, if you've been reading this blog since it started, I am a graduate student. My field is somewhat vague, in that the college I attend (whose name I have carefully left out at my advisor's request) doesn't have a program that exactly fits what I am trying to study. Luckily, after some petitioning (and some all-out begging), I convinced a few professors from a few departments to go to bat for me and defend the accreditation of the field I was trying to pursue, which falls somewhere between New Media Studies and Philosophy. What I wanted to study was the relationship between the self and society / the world / "objective reality," as mediated by the various rivulets of the new media. Meaning, basically: how does the proliferation of an environment in which new media infiltrates nearly every aspect of our lives change the way we perceive ourselves and the broader world?

That may still seem a little vague, but I'm getting to the part where my explanation will start to make sense - the part, in fact, that I've been trying to avoid. Ok, here goes. My theory was that the various channels of the new media (twitter updates on our phones, facebook on our ipods, etc., etc.) have crossed the psychic threshold - the subtle barrier - that mediates the relationship between internal and external reality - the self-enclosed bubble we feel surrounding us, the "force field" beyond which lies everything which is not "myself." This is of note, because (my theory further held) this barrier is a necessary condition of Reason: it is only through this buffer that I am able to consider external circumstances, apply rationality, and pass judgement. Without this buffer - in the face of *immediate* experience - we are only able to react intuitively, instinctually. For example: in the face of attack we instinctually fight or flee, as the situation has breached the buffer between external and internal, and is now threatening the internal "me."

The problem with this is that if I no longer see the external as external - if I instead "feel" that it is an extension of myself - I become accustomed to an environment in which my own consideration is in less demand, and become acclimated to a sort of numbed acceptance of whatever ideas, opinions, or suggestions come across my path: problematic, because of course the external world is a created environment in which factions are constantly working to win converts to their party / idea / brand.

All of which is a bit beside the point for this blog post, because this blog post (and this blog itself) are about the experimentation side of the equation: I needed to see how - for lack of a better word - stupid an idea I could proffer to the masses and still find some sort of following. The acceptance of the idea, I felt, would be indicative of the level to which the mass consideration apparatus had failed. By celebrating and glorifying a man who not only lied to and manipulated millions of people, but did so using his own child, I hoped personally to inspire consideration, judgement, and condemnation, but for the sake of the experiment hoped to inspire allegiance and mute accord. And here you all are.

So I know that now a lot of you must hate my guts, and I can't blame you. I owe you all a big "thank you" for helping me out with my thesis. I hope that being burned twice will make you all a little more wary of what ideas you let inside your heads. I really do feel that the way to peace, prosperity, and social justice is through thoughtful consideration and rationality. Unfortunately, I see the trend moving in the other direction - toward more fear and less thought.

So this will be my final post. Sorry to everyone who is mad at me. Thanks again. - Molly

Rock for Relief - Sold Out

You Searched for: rock for relief tickets
23,231 Results
Search results returned in .13 Seconds

Rock for Relief - Concert Tickets
Rock for Relief tickets available: SOLD OUT... Information: "Rock for Relief is a one-day, five-act summer music festival featuring **Wrath**, **The Battling Nancies**...
www.ticketsplease.com/search/rockforrelief - *see more results like this*

MYTICKETSNOW: rock for relief tickets
Your search for "rock for relief tickets" returned: 0 AVAILABLE. Didn't find what you were looking for? Try our more advanced search...
www.myticketsnow.com/search/rock+for+relief+tickets - *see more results like this*

ROCK FOR RELIEF - TICKETS
Looking for *rock for relief tickets* tickets? Ticket Exchange has them! Even sold out shows! Ticket Exchange always has seats to...
www.ticketexchange.com/search/rockforrelieftickets - *see more results like this*

Page 1 - Next
Searches related to "rock for relief tickets":
Wrath
Battling Nancies
Touchstone
The DeadEye Dolls
The Bastille
Tickets
Rock for Relief
Concert tickets
Summer concert tickets

Search for "rock for relief tickets" in:
Everything
Videos
News
Shopping
More

Disneyland! Yay!!!!

Frank Nevis wrote on the wall for Facebook page **Frank Nevis and the Nevis Family**: Hey everyone! Just getting back home after four great days with the fam in sunny California! The first day I had some meetings so Melissa took the kids to Disneyland by herself. I joined them for the next three days... I will be posting a note about how the meetings went in the next couple of days but for now here are some pictures of our trip to Disneyland... Hope you enjoy (we certainly did)! *1 hour ago*

Frank Nevis created the photo album "Four Days in California" for the Facebook page **Frank Nevis and the Nevis Family**. *1 hour ago*

Frank Nevis added 18 new pictures to the photo album "Four Days in California" *57 minutes ago*

Frank Nevis commented on his photo in the album "Four Days in California": "Back under the Hollywood sign, this time with the whole family!" *55 minutes ago*

Frank Nevis commented on his photo in the album "Four Days in California": "The kids with Mickey and Minnie..." *55 minutes ago*

Frank Nevis commented on his photo in the album "Four Days in California": "Look at those faces! Disneyland! Yay!!!!" *54 minutes ago*

Frank Nevis commented on his photo in the album "Four Days in California": "Ocean sunset enjoyed with the family... what could be better?" *54 minutes ago*

Frank Nevis commented on his photo in the album "Four Days in California": "Back at the airport, ready to fly home... Where does the time go?" *55 minutes ago*

Frank Nevis posted a note to the Facebook page **Frank Nevis and the Nevis Family:** Frank's Trip to California (Part 2) - read more *30 minutes ago*

Frank Nevis commented on his note Frank's Trip to California (Part 2): Here's a rundown of some of what happened when I went to meet with some TV people out in California... *29 minutes ago*

Frank's Trip to California (Part 2)

As the Grateful Dead said, what a long, strange trip it's been!

We got out to California on Wednesday night. Louis had set up some meetings with some TV and cable people (I'm not allowed to say who or which companies) for me for Thursday and Friday morning. Vicki and I thought it would be a great chance to get away with the kids, spend some time together and get away from all of the attention in Missouri. Thursday Vicki took the kids to Disneyland while I went with Louis from meeting to meeting, and then on Friday I met up with the fam for lunch and we went BACK to Disneyland... Saturday and Sunday there as well and then an early flight home Monday morning... A TERRIFIC trip but let me tell you, by the end of it we were all beat, and ready for a vacation from our vacation!

So, I know you're wondering how the meetings went. Thursday started off with a bit of disappointment. We met with a development guy who said that the network he represented was interested in producing an eShow: basically it would be a produced show but shorter than the typical 30 or 60 minute TV block, and shown exclusively on the network's website. He said that it would be bundled into a package of other reality eShows that the company was producing. On the plus side, however, he said that the company loved the premise and wouldn't change a thing about the concept of the show. Louis wants me to seriously consider this option, but something about it is making me hesitate. I don't know. Does anybody watch eShows?

The next meeting was a mixed bag as well. The rep we met with told us that the company was interested in picking up the show in the 30 minute format, but that they wanted to change the concept slightly. The idea they had was that it would be a cross between what we were doing before and Iron Chef: each week the producers of the show would issue a challenge, and I would have five days to invent something that would fit the bill. They were big on the challenge / ticking clock aspect. I don't hate the idea, but I certainly don't love it. Louis says that we have enough interest now that I should find something I am really happy doing, so I'm thinking I'm going to pass on this one.

Next meeting was a little more promising. Sat down with a team of young and very energetic guys who were working on developing shows for their company. They came to the table with a bunch of ideas, and kept asking me if I would be interested in doing a show with all these different kinds of a set ups. It was actually a lot of fun, sitting around and kicking around ideas. One idea they had (which I quickly shut down, don't worry!) was that each week I would invent some sort of transportation ve-hicle - water, land, or air - and that the show would end with one of my kids using it to get from one spot to an-other. They assured me that the whole thing would be su-pervised and totally safe, but I still wasn't ready to sign off on using my kids as crash test dummies! Still, it was great to be in a room with creative people who felt free to throw out any idea. We left there feeling like we might have found a new home.

The last meeting of the day was the shortest of the three, and basically consisted of a rep coming in to talk to me about the nitty-gritty contract details of our potential deal - the company wasn't interested in developing a show, just producing the show we'd already pitched. After spending an hour with the three guys spitballing ideas, it was hard not to feel a little disappointed... Maybe disap-pointed isn't the right word. As we were leaving Louis reminded me that what the guy at the last meeting was trying to give me was exactly what I had been trying to get, and that this guy's demeanor notwithstanding, I should probably take it while it was being offered to me.

Friday morning was, to say the least, the disappointment of the trip. Through some "confusion" the guy we were supposed to be meeting with never showed up. We waited for 45 minutes, with his secretary telling us that he would be down to meet us any second. Oh, well. After we decided not to wait any longer I said goodbye to Louis and headed out to meet the family for lunch. From there it was all onward and upward: no ride at Disneyland was safe from the Nevis clan!

Obviously we have some decisions to make. I will be talking with Vicki, Louis, and the kids. When we make our decision you all will be the first to know. Until then, thank you all for your love and support - we SO appreciate it! Talk to you soon. - Frank

Legal Battle on the Horizon

Legal Battle on the Horizon in Tee-Shirt Quarrel
by Yanni Richards, Staff Writer
www.NationNewsDaily.com/artsandentertainment/articles
/2390239

Jefferson City, MO - The latest legal battle being fought out of the Nevis camp isn't about damages or fraud - it's about merchandise.

"These people have been profiting off of my clients' name, image, and story," said David Green, lawyer for the Nevis family. "We only think it's right that they stop, or that they give my clients what they're entitled to."

"These people" that Mr. Green is referring to are Rich and Margaret Hill of Springfield, Missouri, the owners of GillFallsGirlTees.com, an internet site that sells tee-shirts featuring humorous images and phrases pertaining to the "Gill Falls Girl" incident, in which Frank Nevis falsely claimed that the floodwaters rushing into the town of Gill Falls had carried away his daughter, Melissa. The site proudly boasts that "none of the money [from the sales] goes to Frank and [Frank's wife] Victoria Nevis."

"We understand that people have the right to say, do, and think what they want," said Mr. Green. "That's what makes America great. My clients have no desire to censor the sentiments expressed by Mr. and Mrs. Hill or their products. They do feel, however, that as it is their likeness and story being used, they are entitled to compensation."

The legal action is only the latest volley in what has been a battle of words between the Nevises and the Hills, which began after the public relations firm Harold Brochet and Associates took over the management of the Nevis family's public image. Last month the Nevis family, with the assistance of the firm, launched FrankNevis.com, an internet site devoted to Frank, Victoria, and their children. The site features a "Store" page at which visitors can purchase, among other things, tee-shirts featuring the Nevis family, many of them similar in design and content to those that can be found at GillFallsGirlTees.com.

"They're upset? We're upset," said Rich Hill. "They stole our designs and started saying that their site was the only place to get "official" merchandise. It's official all right: it's officially stolen."

So far the exchange has consisted only of strongly-worded emails from Victoria Nevis to the Hills, asking them to take down their site. These emails, she said, have met with no response. That changed Monday, when the

Nevises asked Mr. Green to issue an official cease-and-desist request. Only time will tell if the request will have its desired effect, but as of this writing GillFallsGirl Tees.com was still online and still offering the Hills' products, with no indication that they would be shutting down.

Yanni Richards is a Staff Writer for NationNewsDaily. com. Contact Yanni directly at YanniRichards@National-News Daily.com.

Frank Nevis posted a link

Frank Nevis posted a link on the wall for Facebook page **Frank Nevis and the Nevis Family**: *www.Frank Nevis.com/TheNevisFamilyintheNews.html 12 hours ago*

Frank Nevis commented on his post: VERY EXCITING NEWS! Click the link to get to our "News" page, where you can find out all the latest. It's finally happening!!!!!! :) *12 hours ago*

THE NEVIS FAMILY IN THE NEWS

LATEST NEWS: Frank Nevis Inks Deal with Hobart Entertainment, "The Invention of Family 2.0" Slated for Fall Lineup *www.thescoop.com/articles/209324*

Frank talks to Phil Tanner of Talk Nation. Click the link below to watch a clip and read commentary.

www.NationalNewsNetwork.com/programs/talknation/ep2
93/clip1

Frank talks to Greg Morgan. Click the link to watch the full interview. _www.youtube.com/user/wnn/greg morganinterviewsgranknevis?blend=1&ob=5#p/f/ 2/8c6tcrwwTto_

www.TheScoop.com/articles/209324

Frank Nevis Inks Deal with Hobart Entertainment, The Invention of Family 2.0 Slated for Fall Lineup
by Tammy Folger, Staff Writer
www.thescoop.com/articles/209324

Frank Nevis, patriarch of the now-famous Nevis family, has inked a deal with Hobart Entertainment, the company behind the hit reality shows _Dumpster Kings_ and _Beyond the Pale: My Albino Life._

The show will begin filming this summer, and will feature Frank Nevis, his wife Victoria, and their five children Sandra (11), Billy (10), June (8), Tommy (7), and Melissa (6), as well as occasional appearances by Victoria's mother Barbara Lagrange, famous for publicly declaring that the "Gill Falls Girl" incident was, in fact, an elaborate hoax. Each week Frank will be presented with a task requiring an invention, and materials with which to build a prototype.

"We like to call it a cross between *Iron Chef* and Einstein," says Dave Gruin, executive director of Hobart Entertainment. He added, "We're very excited to work with Frank, and very excited about this new show."

The Nevis family was involved in an earlier incarnation of the show. Entitled *The Invention of Family,* the original show followed Frank Nevis in his efforts to make a career as an inventor while juggling the demands of family life. A pilot was produced, but the show was not picked up for syndication.

The Invention of Family 2.0 is slated to premiere this fall on the reality network RealLifeTV, the parent company of Hobart Entertainment.

Tammy Folger is a Staff Writer for TheScoop.com. Contact her at tfolger@thescoop.com. Subscribe to The Scoop by sending an email to subscribe@thescoop.com.

Gorgon Records, Inc. wrote on their own wall

Gorgon Records, Inc. wrote on their own wall: Only 11 MORE DAYS until ROCK FOR RELIEF!!! The show is SOLD OUT, but you can win a pair of tickets by sending us a Facebook message explaining why YOU should be the one to win! Winner announced in one week! *10 days ago 14 likes*

Gorgon Records, Inc. wrote on their own wall: Only 10 MORE DAYS until ROCK FOR RELIEF!! Be sure to enter to win a pair of tickets to this SOLD OUT show by sending us a pm saying why you should win! Wrath, The

Battling Nancies, The DeadEye Dolls, The Bastille, and Touchstone... 12 HOURS OF ROCK AND ROLL!!!! *9 days ago 32 likes*

Gorgon Records, Inc. wrote on their own wall: 9 MORE F*CKING DAYS!!! *8 days ago 19 likes*

Gorgon Records, Inc. wrote on their own wall: 8 MORE DAYS until the Rock for Relief one-day, five-band music spectacular EXPLODES on Jefferson City! Win two tickets to this SOLD OUT show by writing in and telling us why YOU should be the winner! *7 days ago 8 likes*

Gorgon Records, Inc. wrote on their own wall: "People forget that Rock and Roll is about love, it's about community, it's about helping each other out. If it's all hate and anger, that's not Rock and Roll." - Jarett Biarero of WRATH... See Wrath in 7 MORE DAYS at the ROCK FOR RELIEF!!! *6 days ago 27 likes*

Gorgon Records, Inc. wrote on their own wall: There's still time to enter to win tickets to the SOLD OUT Rock for Relief summer music festival... PM us and tell us why you should be the one who wins the tickets *5 days ago 23 likes*

Gorgon Records, Inc. wrote on their own wall: Wrath, Touchstone, The Battling Nancies, the DeadEye Dolls, and The Bastille, plus a special SURPRISE GUEST!!! 5 MORE DAYS!!!! *4 days ago 14 likes*

Gorgon Records, Inc. wrote on their own wall: CONGRATULATIONS to Bryan Hart of Blue Springs, Missouri! Jason wrote in and told us that he should win the two tickets to the Rock for Relief summer music festival, and we agreed! Jason's winning entry is available for you to read in our notes, click on WHY I SHOULD WIN by Bryan Hart *3 days ago 13 likes*

Gorgon Records, Inc. wrote on their own wall: 3 MORE DAYS!!!! WRATH, TOUCHSTONE, THE BATTLING NANCIES, THE DEADEYE DOLLS, THE BASTILLE PLUS A SPECIAL SURPRISE GUEST!!! *2 days ago 42 likes*

Gorgon Records, Inc. wrote on their own wall: ONLY 2 MORE DAYS!!!!! Jefferson City won't know what hit it!!!!! *1 day ago 24 likes*

Gorgon Records, Inc. wrote on their own wall: 1 MORE DAY!!!! *12 hours ago 54 likes*

Why I Should Win by Bryan Hart

I should win because I have never been to a rock and roll concert. My parents are very religious, and they won't let me go to rock shows. They think rock and roll makes people bad, even though I try to explain to them that rock and roll is good, that it brings people together and helps them understand each other. I have to hide all of my CDs and the only way I can get new music is my friend Greg gets music and then renames it all when he downloads it onto his computer, and gives it the names of Christian bands that my parents think is OK... Then I give him my iPod at school and he puts the new stuff on there for me.

I was talking to my parents the other day, trying to tell them that Rock and Roll isn't bad. I brought up the Rock for Relief concert, to try to say, Look, all of these rock musicians are getting together and trying to help the people whose homes were destroyed by the flooding. How can it be bad if all they're trying to do is help people they don't even know? Isn't that what Jesus would do? I told them that the show was sold out and everything, but I got them to say that if the show wasn't sold out they would let me go. They thought it was ok to say that, because they thought I wouldn't be able to get a ticket. If I win the two tickets, they will have to let me go, and I will take my friend Greg as a way of saying "thank you" for going through all this trouble to share new music with me. Honestly, it has saved my life. I don't know what I would do if I didn't have this music. I would lose my mind living in my house.

Please please please consider making me the winner.

RealLifeTV.com/shows/The_Invention_of_Family_2.0

www.RealLifeTV.com/show/The_Invention_of_Family_2.0

RealLifeTV is very excited to announce a new show for our fall lineup, *The Invention of Family 2.0*. This 1-hour show will follow inventor Frank Nevis as he works to complete weekly challenges, at the same time juggling the demands of family life with his wife Victoria and their five children.

"We like to think of it as a cross between *Iron Chef* and Einstein," says Dave Gruin, executive director of Hobart Entertainment, the production company handling the show. He adds, "We're very excited to work with Frank, and very excited about this new show."

Each week Frank will be presented with a challenge which he must resolve by inventing a device using materials provided him. (Have a great idea for a weekly challenge for Frank? Submit it on our forum by clicking here. Your suggestion may be used!)

RealLifeTV is excited to welcome the Nevis family to their new home on RLTV.

RealLifeTV.com/forum/topic/The_Invention_of_Family_2.0

Not a member yet? Register by clicking here.

Topic: What sort of challenges would you like to see Frank Nevis presented with on the new RLTV show *The Invention of Family 2.0*?
posted by: RealLifeTV

What sort of challenges would you like to see Frank Nevis presented with on the new RLTV show *The Invention of Family 2.0*? We will be using suggestions from this forum when scripting the show so be sure to watch, the suggestion we use may be yours!

Reply 1
posted by: TomBillings

I think it would be a real challenge for Frank to not come off as a self-promoting douchebag. Maybe he could invent something that would help with that.

Reply 2
posted by: MarkEasly

It drives me nuts that I can't cut the grass between my fenceposts. There's always just a little bit of grass that's a little bit too high. I know I can use the weed whacker, but I hate that I have to get off the lawn mower and go all the way back to the garage to get it. Maybe he could make some sort of mechanical attachment, like on a vacuum, that would get in between there. Thanks. Hope you use my suggestion.

Reply 3
posted by: DavidJenkins

I put all of my dirty dishes into the sink, fill the sink with soap and water, reach in to pull the dishes out and start washing them. Problem is that I often have sharp knives in the sink, and don't know where they are until I feel them. I haven't been cut yet, but I'm sure one day I'm going to get cut. Maybe Frank could invent something that would fix this problem.

Reply 4
posted by: LeslieGeller

I keep locking my keys in my car. I feel like with automatic door locks it should be pretty easy to have some sort of detector, that wouldn't let the doors lock when the keys were inside the car.

Reply 5
posted by: RichardMiller

I agree with post # 1

Reply 6
posted by: PeterHudnut

Maybe he could invent a way for his children to be completely screwed up for life... no wait, this whole debacle should pretty much do it. never mind.

Reply 7
posted by: CarrieNaris

my bras get tangled when i put them in the dryer... maybe frank could come up with some way to store them so they wont get tangled thanx

---

"Surprise Guest" Causes Uproar: A Snafu in Review

Surprise Guest Causes Uproar: A Snafu in Review
by Grant Haight, guest contributor
www.MUSICNOW!.com/article/12949

Jefferson City, MO - Sex, booze, drugs, and mayhem: everything was going fine at Gorgon Records, Inc.'s summer music festival **Rock for Relief,** held yesterday and last night in Jefferson City. Everything was going fine, that is, until the powers that be decided to unveil their "Surprise Guest."

"We're going to bring this guy out here now," said Jarett Biarero of **Wrath**, the show's headlining act. "I don't know what's going to happen," he added. "Things might get crazy."

And things did get crazy, when who should walk out from the wings but Frank Nevis, hoax-master extraordinaire and the star of RealLifeTV's new reality series **The Invention of Family 2.0**. A few "bro hugs" for the band members later Frank was front and center with a microphone in his hand.

"This is crazy," he said, wearing a smile on his face that indicated to this reporter that he was unaware of the crowd's rapidly darkening humor. "It's great that you all came out today to see these guys and to support **Rock for Relief**. A lot of you know that my town, Gill Falls, was pretty much destroyed by flooding a few months ago, and there were a bunch of other towns -,"

At this point it became difficult for me, standing near the stage, to hear what Frank was saying over the "boos" and shouts from the crowd. Frank continued speaking for several moments before he paused, apparently waiting for the crowd to quiet down. When it became clear that they had no intention of quieting he offered the mic to Jarrett Biarero, an offer which the **Wrath** frontman declined by turning his back on the TV star.

"I know," Frank began again, this time shouting into the microphone, making himself marginally audible, "I know that a lot of you don't like me." (This line alone earned the crowd's brief approval.) "You can feel about me however you want, but I'm here today as a resident of Gill Falls, as a person whose life was changed by the flooding, and I want to say "Thank You" on behalf of all of the Missourians you are helping by being here today."

The first plastic water bottle that came onto the stage appeared to be only half-full, and when it struck Frank it seemed to surprise him more than hurt him. The several dozen that quickly followed, however, dispelled any lingering uncertainty about the crowd's feelings and quickly transformed the stage into something resembling a New Jersey junk barge. Frank, obviously angered, made one final attempt to address the crowd before Jarret Biarero and a pair of security personnel ushered him unceremoniously from the line of fire.

"All right, settle it on down," said Biarero, returning to the microphone. Even so, it took ten minutes before the hail of bottles and other debris stopped entirely, giving this reporter the impression that perhaps the crowd's animosity was in fact venting itself upon the band, not just the retreating memory of Frank Nevis. Right or wrong, it did seem that **Wrath** had become the proxy for the event's organizers at Gorgon Records, Inc., and was taking the blame for their bad move.

Which leads me to the real question at the heart of this thing: Why would anyone anywhere schedule or hire Frank Nevis to appear as a special surprise guest? Despite the crafted presentation - the appearance - of celebrity (look at Frank's website or Facebook page and you might think he was a star) this reporter's sense - especially after witnessing the debacle at **Rock for Relief** - is that people genuinely don't like Frank Nevis, no matter how much he is rebranded and shoved down their throats. Now I don't mean to pick a side in the always-heated debate about celebrity in America, and I am certain that a very compelling argument could be made that one doesn't have to be liked to become famous, or even successful. There are plenty of people who are famous because we love to dislike - if not outright revile - them. Still, my sense is that people are simply done with Frank Nevis: that his tireless efforts to pull on our coattails and stay in the periphery of our cultural consciousness have become obnoxious and boring, and we would all rather just see him go away. I could be wrong, but what I felt from the crowd last night was less displeasure and more annoyance that their music - and their lives - had been interrupted by this self-promoting and self-aggrandizing weasel, and that all they really wanted was for him to just go away and stop bothering them.

Whether because they tired of throwing things or just ran out of ammunition the crowd's volley soon abated, and **Wrath** resumed their set with great gusto. Frank Nevis's appearance didn't ruin the festival - I wouldn't even say that it defined, in any way, the headliner's act. It was just a momentary annoyance, quickly and gladly forgotten - perhaps an indication of things to come.

Grant Haight is a frequent contributor to MUSICNOW! Contact him at GrantHaight@MusicNow.com.

Ryan McIntosh wrote...

Ryan McIntosh wrote on his own wall: BEST F'ING CONCERT EVER battling nancies touchstone WRATH F*CKING KILLED IT so happy now going to sleep *17 hours ago 12 comments 5 likes*

Ryan McIntosh commented on his post: p.s. frank nevis is a f*cking douchebag and i hope his show gets cancelled after the first episode... *17 hours ago 7 likes*

Hal Vincent commented on Ryan McIntosh's post: yeah I heard he got up on stage during the concert... wtf is that about? *17 hours ago*

Ryan McIntosh commented on his own post: @Hal yeah they brought him out on stage during Wrath's set... he started trying to say something about thanks for doing this for the flood victims before everybody started booing too loud for him to talk lol *17 hours ago*

Luke Paul commented on Ryan McIntosh's post: i was there too my buddy threw the first bottle that hit him it was f'ing classic i was laughing so hard that guy is such a tool *17 hours ago 5 likes*

Ryan McIntosh commented on his own post: @Luke tell your buddy that was an amazing shot my hat is off to him lol *17 hours ago*

Tim Lukens commented on Ryan McIntosh's post: CLASSIC *17 hours ago*

Erin Blake commented on Ryan McIntosh's post: im kinda looking forward to that show but i don't think it will be on the air for very long people really hate that guy i think it will be interesting seeing what he invents *16 hours ago*

Ryan McIntosh commented on his own post: @Erin he should invent a time machine so he can go back and stop himself from telling everyone his kid went over the falls... he was a nobody but at least nobody hated him *16 hours ago*

Rick Duke commented on Ryan McIntosh's post: this whole situation has become so bizarre... only in america *16 hours ago*

Eli Newel commented on Ryan McIntosh's post: @Rick GOD BLESS THE USA LOL *16 hours ago*

Ryan McIntosh commented on his own post: *www.YouTube.com/user/bigwillystyle12/franknevishitwith bottle?blend=1&ob=5#p/f/2/8c6tcrwwTto* cell phone video of frank nevis getting hit with a bottle at rock for relief... funniest shit i've ever sen *15 hours ago*

Ryan McIntosh commented on his own post: *seen *15 hours ago*

The rumor mill is working overtime

Hello and welcome to The Daily Dish, your one-stop-shop for all the latest in celebrity and pop culture news. Well the rumor mill is working overtime, and the news is all bad for Frank Nevis and the much-ballyhooed Nevis family. According to an inside source, RealLifeTV is thinking of dropping the just-greenlit reality show *The Invention of Family 2.0* from it's lineup, which would have starred the Nevis family and was scheduled for a fall premiere. According to our source, the change in plans is coming as a result of Frank Nevis's unfortunate appearance at the *Rock for Relief* music festival in Jefferson City, Missouri last week, at which unruly and unwelcoming fans showered Nevis and the stage with insults, bottles, and other garbage - not exactly a subtle review. No word as yet if RealLifeTV has shut down production of the show as well, which was being handled by their subsidiary Hobart Entertainment. As always we will have all the latest on this developing story as it comes to us...

Nevis Family Show Moved to Web...

Nevis Family Show Moved to Web; Nevis Family Considering Litigation
by Bill Hodgeman, Staff Writer

In a somewhat unsurprising move the reality show network RealLifeTV has begun to hedge their bets regarding the Nevis family and their reality show, *The Invention of Family 2.0.* Execs at the network announced this week that the 1-hour show would be trimmed to 30 minutes, and would appear as a series of weekly "webisodes" on the network's website.

"The fact of the matter is that we have a lot of terrific shows in the fall lineup, a lot more than would fit in the primetime hours. Some shuffling had to be done," said George Pole, Executive Vice President of Scheduling at RealLifeTV. He added, "I want to make it very clear that this is not a reflection on *The Invention of Family 2.0*, which we feel is going to be a terrific and very entertaining show."

Despite Mr. Pole's upbeat tone, Nevis family lawyer David Green said that his clients don't consider the move a simple matter of scheduling.

"They're very upset," said Mr. Green. "I don't know how else to put it. They're very, very upset. This move is obviously a response to the events at last week's music festival, which we certainly feel is not a fair indication of the public's feelings toward my clients." He added, "We are certainly considering legal action. My clients have a contract with RealLifeTV which explicitly states the nature of both the production and distribution of content starring my clients. We are most definitely considering legal action."

Litigation may have to wait, however, until more pressing matters have been resolved: this week a coalition of Gill Falls residents filed a suit against the Nevis family, claiming that they are entitled to a portion of the profits the Nevis family has received through the free and exploitive use of the town and its residents.

Bill Hodgeman is a Staff Writer for the Daily Post-Tribune. Contact him directly at BHodgeman@DailyPost Tribune.com. This article is available online at www.Daily PostTribune.com.

From: donotreply@franknevis.com
To: mailinglist@franknevis.com
Subject: The Nevis Family Newsletter #2

Hello Again,

As I'm sure some of you already know from watching the news and following the various goings on with us, it has been a busy, busy couple of months for the Nevis Family. I'll start with all the good things (accentuate the positive!) and leave the unhappy stuff for last...

A lot of you probably know that the biggest thing happening with us is that Frank signed a deal with Hobart Entertainment and RealLifeTV to get "The Invention of Family" back into production! This is by far the biggest news, and all of the other bad news just fades away when I think about it. After school let out we all went out to California and Frank and Louis (our agent from Harold Brochet and Assoc.) had a bunch of meetings with TV people. The kids and I went to Disneyland (the kids LOVED it, no surprise there) and then Frank met up with us later. When we got back Frank got a call from Hobart Entertainment that they were ready to make a deal, and we hopped back on a plane and signed! This version of the show is going to be a little bit different than the first one: the producers are going to give Frank a challenge each week and he's going to have to invent something to deal with the challenge. It should be a lot of fun, and we're really looking forward to filming it!

In other terrific news, Frank and I sat down with a realtor yesterday and PUT A DOWN PAYMENT ON A HOUSE IN SUNNY SOUTHERN CALIFORNIA!!!! While we were out in LA to sign the deal with Hobart we went to look at a couple of houses and just absolutely fell in love with one. Frank says that he is going to post some pictures on the Facebook page when he gets a chance, so keep your eyes peeled for those - they should be up soon.

Now on to the bad news...

We got word from the network last week that the show is not going to be shown on the network, but is going to be viewable on their website instead. Needless to say, we were disappointed. Louis says that contractually we are guaranteed airtime, and that there is some ambiguity that may let us insist that we are guaranteed time on the network, but he says it could go either way depending on how the judge reads it, if we decide to go to court over it. So we're still thinking about that one. Part of me thinks that really having the show viewable online only isn't even a problem: plenty of people watch TV on their computers. I guess the thing that makes me nervous is that they seem to be losing their enthusiasm for the show... I hope I'm just reading too much into it.

In other bad news, our neighbors are suing us for using the town of Gill Falls for our own economic gain without paying them for the right to do so... I know, it's as crazy as it sounds. David, our lawyer, says that it's just a publicity thing and that the lawyer they've got representing them is famous for pulling these kinds of stunts. He says they don't have a case and I trust him, but I'll feel a lot better when it's settled.

The movers are coming this afternoon - everything is happening so fast! Frank and I are so lucky and no matter whatever else happens we never lose sight of that fact. Thank you all for your love and support.

Lots of love to everyone out there from all of us here.
Vicki & the Fam.

"God bless Frank Nevis"

Forget Frank Nevis: It's Gill Falls That's Open for Business
by Terry Goulet, Staff Writer
www.MissouriRegister.com/article/gillfallsopenbusiness

It's hard to believe that it's already been four months since the now-infamous "Gill Falls Girl" prank that propelled Frank Nevis toward reality television stardom and the town of Gill Falls into the national spotlight. Hard to believe, that its, unless you're standing on Main Street in Gill Falls and can see the nearly miraculous transformation that those four months have brought.

"We've been working hard," says Grant Niare, newly-elected Chair of the newly-formed Gill Falls Business Council. "We've done just about everything you could possibly do in four months and now we're back, we're ready, we're open for business."

The business Mr. Niare is referring to is all centered around the unexpected influx of tourists pouring into Gill Falls.

"It's crazy," says Betty Drier, owner of Betty's Diner, a fixture of the Main Street strip. "Every weekend we're packed to the gills. I have people waiting for tables. I've been open for thirty years, and I don't think I've ever had anyone wait for a table."

She's not complaining. Neither is Bob Jeffries, owner of Bob's Bait & Tackle, a fishing and souvenir shop.

"I've never sold so many Gill Falls tee-shirts," he says. "I actually sold out. I've had those shirts on the shelves for years."

What's true for diners and bait and tackle shops is true for the whole town: every business has seen a sudden upswing in patronage and profits.

"Truth be told, people have been coming in since before I was even back open for business," says Bob Jeffries. "The crowd went from volunteers helping with the cleanup to people looking to shop and spend money. There has been a crowd in town ever since the flood happened."

No one is trying too hard to pin down the reason for their new success, but if pressed many will point to the exposure given to the town by Frank and Victoria Nevis.

"Like it or not, their antics have put us on the map," says Grant Niare. "People want to see where it all happened. I think some of them also feel like we got a raw deal in the whole thing, and they want to help us out."

Mr. Niare, for his part, is doing his best to encourage their patronage. In his new role as Chair of the Business Council he has petitioned the state for a special tax exemption, in light of the recovery efforts, that allows local businesses to sell their goods sales-tax free, creating an incentive to shop in Gill Falls. He has also worked with local law enforcement to suspend open container laws.

"We're not trying to create Mardi Gras out here," he adds. "But people like to sit out on the patios outside these restaurants and enjoy a glass of wine or a beer. It creates a friendly, relaxed atmosphere."

When asked what he thinks the long term prospects are for Gill Falls as a tourist draw, Mr. Niare is full of ideas.

"I'm envisioning an annual festival," he says. "Rides in the park, food venders along Main Street, and a model boat race down the river."

"I hate to say it, but God bless Frank Nevis," laughs Tootsie Baker, a lifelong Gill Falls resident and owner of Baker's Beauty Salon. "Reality show or not, I think we're the ones who are really going to win out in the end."

Terry Goulet is a Staff Writer for the Missouri Register. Contact Terry directly at TGoulet@MissouriRegister.com. A print version of this issue is available at www.Missouri Register.com/contact/subscriptions.

Tonight on RealLifeTV.com

www.RealLifeTV.com/show/The_Invention_of_Family_2.0

Tonight! Don't miss the highly-anticipated debut of **The Invention of Family 2.0**, available exclusively as a free webisode on RealLifeTV.com! Frank tries to come up with a device to automatically replace the toilet paper when it runs out; Vicki takes the kids shopping.

Frank Nevis wrote...

Frank Nevis wrote on the wall for the Facebook page **Frank Nevis and the Nevis Family**: The Invention of Family 2.0 DEBUTS TONIGHT! We've been working very hard and are very excited for the premiere. Hope you tune in and enjoy! Point your web browser to *www.RealLifeTV.com/show/The_Invention_of_Family_2.0* at 7:30... It's FREE! *2 hours ago*

About *@FrankNevis*

2398 Tweets / 595 Following / 23,493 Followers / 230 Listed

Bio: Frank Nevis is a father, inventor, and TV personality. Find out more about him at www.FrankNevis.com

@FrankNevis

> The Invention of Family 2.0 debuts TONIGHT! Tune in to RealLifeTV.com at 7:30! *3 hours ago*

@FrankNevis

> Long day of filming... Outback for dinner with the fam and then home to sleep! *18 hours ago*

@FrankNevis

> Anyone know where to find a socket wrench at this hour in west L.A.? *20 hours ago*

@FrankNevis

> Just got some of the new furniture delivered... Vicki isn't sure she likes it but I have had it with furniture shopping! Who knew moving was so exhausting? *2 days ago*

@FrankNevis

> Getting settled in the new house... Kids have picked rooms and aren't just sleeping in a pile in the living room anymore :) *4 days ago*

Aren't we done with these people yet?

*www.watchout.com/forum/franknevis/topic/theinventio
noffamily2.0/episode1*

Topic: The Invention of Family...
posted by: RobRider28 *1 hour ago*

So can we all agree that that was the worst half-hour of television - excuse me, "compu-vision" - that we have ever seen? I appreciate that one episode was necessary to help us understand why Frank Nevis never made it as an inventor (he's incompetent) but beyond that I can't see the point in much more of this... I, for one, am still shocked that anyone signed on to produce this show in the first place. Maybe I'm wrong, but I will be surprised if this lasts the season (or however they break up syndication in "compu-vision" land). I mean really: AREN'T WE DONE WITH THESE PEOPLE YET?

Reply 1
posted by: DanDover *55 minutes ago*

While I do typically feel that it is unfair to judge a show based on a single episode, there did not seem to be much redeeming in this series' first offering... I think the thing I found the most surprising / disturbing was the lack of chemistry between Frank and Victoria... I mean I realize that personal chemistry doesn't always translate to onscreen chemistry, but come on... This was like watching two fourteen-year-olds at a middle school dance.

Reply 2
posted by: PamLawler *53 minutes ago*

I agree with Dan: HORRIBLE onscreen chemistry. They've been working so hard to get on-camera and now that they are it's like they don't know what to do with themselves. Whoever is producing this show needs to get them some acting coaches QUICK, if only for the sake of screen presence.

Reply 3
posted by: HillaryTurner *49 minutes ago*

And their poor children are like sheep or something... did anyone else find it totally disturbing the way the kids just walked around like they were in a daze?

Reply 4
posted by: LaurenGocher *43 minutes ago*

@Hillary: I TOTALLY agree... Those kids looked drugged or horrified or something, and Frank and Victoria just kept dragging them... I've said it before and I'm worried that I'll have to say it again (and again, and again): these people are sick and should not be trusted with the care of children. Have we all forgotten how this whole thing started?

Reply 5
posted by: TuckerBruce *41 minutes ago*

...All of which doesn't even begin to mention the fact that FRANK'S INVENTION DIDN'T WORK!

Reply 6
posted by: JeremyMontrose *37 minutes ago*

@Tucker: LOL

Reply 7
posted by: WillCarter *33 minutes ago*

I give it three episodes. After three they'll realize that despite the production costs this turkey isn't worth the bandwidth it takes to broadcast it.

WATCH OUT! is a community discussion forum. It is our belief that much of the world's news is kept from U.S. audiences, and that to know what is really going on in the world we must look beyond the (domestically-based) so-called "World News" Networks. This is a place for the free exchange of information and ideas.

Not a member yet? Register by clicking <u>here</u>.

Like watching a child bake

Hello and welcome to The Daily Dish, your one-stop-shop for all the latest in celebrity and pop culture news. Well webisode one of the new reality series "The Invention of Family 2.0" is in the books and the reviews are in. Last night nearly eight million Americans plunked down in front of their computer screens and logged on to watch Frank and Victoria Nevis wrestle with problems ranging from mechanical malfunction to unmatching kids' socks, then they hit Twitter, Facebook, and the blogosphere to give their two cents. Username MoonRiver tweeted at DailyDish: "I haven't seen a family dynamic that awkward and uncomfortable since my boyfriend's family reunion." Carrie Howland wrote on our Facebook wall, saying, "Watching Frank invent is like watching a child bake: it's cute how hard he's trying, but you're not surprised when all you're left with is a mess." And blogger PixieMinx wrote on her blog: "I just watched *The Invention of Family 2.0*... I have been trying to figure out what to say about it, what aspect to comment on, and have come to the conclusion that the only thing to say is that this show simply does not work. No chemistry, no interest, no reason for being." Well you heard it here, folks, straight from the horse's mouth. No word from RealLifeTV yet what they plan to do with the show, but Frank and Victoria: maybe you shouldn't sell that home in Gill Falls just yet.

Truth Falls

---

www.MilestonesNetwork.com/News

Milestones Network is pleased to announce the newest project to be greenlit by our award-winning in-house production company, Milestones Pictures. *Truth Falls* is the story of Bob and Melinda Davis, a couple living in Truth Falls, Mississippi. When the town is threatened by flooding from the swollen Mississippi River, out-of-work Bob hatches a desperate plan: hide their five-year-old son with Bob's mother in a neighboring town and tell the authorities he was carried away by the floodwaters. Soon the waters are bearing down on Bob and Melinda's home and with them, the scrutiny of a nation captivated by Bob and Melinda's story. But how long can they maintain the lie, before *Truth Falls*? Starring Chris O'Donnell as Bob Davis and Cameron Diaz as Melinda Davis, *Truth Falls* will premiere this December, exclusively on Milestones.

Motion Dismissed

Motion Dismissed; Gill Falls v. Nevis Family Moves Forward
by Phil Rebbing, court reporter
www.JeffersonCityTribune.com/news/courtnotices/923320

Jefferson City, MO - Judge Ruth Thompson ruled this week against a motion to dismiss submitted by David Green, lawyer for the Nevis family, that would have ended litigation in the case brought by residents of the Nevises' former hometown of Gill Falls, Missouri.

"We are very happy that the case is moving forward," said Harry Cooper, one of the lawyers representing the residents of Gill Falls. "We strongly feel that the Nevises have profited at these people's expense. We only want what's fair."

What's fair, according to papers filed by the residents of Gill Falls, is up to half of the income generated by the reality show in which the Nevises are currently starring. Entitled *The Invention of Family 2.0*, the show follows Frank, a would-be inventor, as he works to juggle family demands and complete challenges laid out by the show's producers. The show, and the Nevises' fame, is the direct result of a widely-publicized prank perpetuated by the Nevises on the residents of Gill Falls during flooding there six months ago - or at least that is the claim laid out in the case brought by Cooper, his colleagues, and their clients.

However, despite the ruling, the Nevis camp is far from throwing in the towel.

"This case is ludicrous," said David Green, lawyer for the Nevis family. "The town and the people of Gill Falls were, at most, a backdrop for the events in question. By the same logic the prosecution is employing we might say that the entire state of Missouri - or even the entire country - has the same right to recompense. Where does it stop?" He added simply, "Their case doesn't stand a chance."

Only time will tell, and parties on both sides will have to wait, as Judge Thompson ruled in favor of a continuance that would postpone the upcoming trial to allow the Nevises to return to work on *The Invention of Family 2.0*.

Phil Rebbing is a regular contributor to the Jefferson City Tribune. Contact him directly at PhilRebbing@Jefferson CityTribune.com. A subscription to the print version of this newspaper is available at www.JeffersonCityTribune .com/print/subscriptions

Quietly limping

....And in other Daily Dish news, last night saw webisode two of the Nevis-family-centered reality show *The Invention of Family 2.0* quietly limping across fiber optic cables to about two million American viewers. For those of you paying attention or keeping track that's a five million viewer drop-off - just about the steepest we've ever seen. Frank Nevis was quick to point out on the Nevis Family's Facebook page that these numbers may not be significant, as ratings are hard to tabulate for on-demand, online content. Sure thing, Frank. No word yet from ReaLifeTV as to plans for the show, but advertising for the show was noticeably absent from their website this morning, almost as though it was pulled the second the ratings came in... Never a good sign. In other Nevis family news Frank's invention from last week, the automatic toilet paper refilleramajig, just went on sale on FrankNevis.com, a fact Frank mentioned a number of times in last night's webisode, in a show of calculated cross-promotion so artless it will probably do more to hamper the product's already abysmal sales. I'm sure it doesn't help anything that Frank never got the thing to work quite right on last week's episode. More on this nosedive as it comes to us...

Elephant Smell

The Invention of Family 2.0 Production Halted, Re maining Episodes to Air
by Pauline Mollier, guest contributor
www.thenewshound.com/entertainment/article2139

Just two "webisodes" in and Hobart Entertainment has pulled the plug on *The Invention of Family 2.0.* In a statement released to news groups this morning, Hobart Entertainment executive Ron Ernest said that the production company "is looking for ways to cut costs" and that "the shutdown is potentially temporary."

"The future of *The Invention of Family 2.0* is dependent on its performance with viewers, on their verdict, just like the future of every other show," he said. He went on to explain that Hobart Entertainment's parent company RealLifeTV would air the remaining three episodes that had been completed before the shutdown, and decide based on their performance whether to resume production. (Read Mr. Ernest's full statement here.)

Despite the phenomenon in recent years of cancelled shows being resurrected through the adamance of diehard fans, one gets the sense that such will not be the case with *The Invention of Family 2.0.* Seven months in the spotlight is a decent run, and is more than most people get. But a quick look around the web shows you the state of things: the only posts in recent weeks on the Nevis Family Facebook page are from Frank or Victoria; the forum chatter has all but died out; Frank's Twitter followers don't seem to be re-tweeting his posts with the frequency they once did. As one blogger nicely summed it up: "public interest in the Nevis Family has run it's course. The circus draws a crowd, but only because it doesn't stay in one place for two long. If it doesn't leave, pretty soon nobody goes to see it and everyone is sick of the elephant smell."

I think everybody feels that it's about time for this circus to hit the road.

Pauline Mollier is a frequent contributor to the Arts & Entertainment section of The News Hound Online. Contact her directly at PMollier@NewsHound.com.

The Nevis Family Newsletter #3

From: donotreply@franknevis.com

To: mailinglist@franknevis.com
Subject: The Nevis Family Newsletter #3

Hello All,

First of all, Frank and I want to give a big THANK YOU to all of you who have supported us through these ups and downs. Whenever things are looking badly for us we always remind each other that there are people out there who care about us, that we have an extended family now and that we are very blessed. So thank you all for being in our lives and for giving us a reason to keep moving forward when things are looking down.

As I'm sure you've all heard by now, Hobart Entertainment has shut down production of the show. This was done in response to the drop-off in ratings between the first and second episodes. We filmed five total, and the people at RealLifeTV are going to air the rest of them and decide whether to start production up again based on how those perform. Episode three aired last night, and the ratings drop wasn't nearly as big as the one between one and two, and so we're hoping that if the ratings can stay steady through the next two that we can get back to work. So please please please tell your friends to watch the show!

In other news, our former neighbors are suing us. That's right, they're suing us. The good people of Gill Falls are saying that they deserve compensation for the part they played in this whole thing. I can't even talk about it, it makes me so mad. David (our lawyer) says that they don't have a case and that he is handling it, and I have complete faith in him so I just have to remember to take a few deep breaths...

There, much better. All that aside, the new house is terrific, and the kids love California. With or without the show, this was the right move for us. We are SO much happier here. This is where we belong, and if nothing else comes of this in the long run then it will be enough that it brought us out here.

That's all for this time. Please please please tell your friends, your family, strangers on the street, TELL EVE-RYBODY to click on to RealLifeTV.com Thursday nights at 7:30 to see new episodes of *The Invention of Family 2.0*, or RealLifeTV anytime to see past episodes on-demand. With your help, we can keep the show going!

Sending you all much gratitude. Lots of love to all of you out there from all of us here.

Vicki & the Fam.

Tonight on Talk Nation

Hello and welcome to Talk Nation. I'm your host, Richard Becker, and my guest tonight is Dr. David Sellers, professor of Media and Cultural Studies at Whitlock College and the author of the new book *MediaFrenzy: How the New Media Feeding Frenzy is Destroying America.* Dr. Sellers, welcome to the show.

Thank you, Richard. Thank you for having me.

So Dr. Sellers you had the idea for this book a year ago and if I'm not mistaken it started as an article -

That's right.

- that you wrote for Anvil Magazine. If you would, tell us just briefly what that article said.

Certainly. Uh, well I wrote that piece for Anvil at the height of the, I guess I would call it - if I can quote myself - "news frenzy" surrounding Frank and Victoria Nevis who as your viewers may recall told authorities that their six-year-old daughter had been carried away by the flooding that was going on at that time and who they subsequently claimed or allowed everyone to believe had been carried over the Gill Falls Waterfall some five miles downstream.

I don't think there is any danger of anyone forgetting that any time soon.

No most likely not, and most likely they will not because of what I wrote about in the article, which was that when the flooding occurred there were already newspeople standing by on the scene, hoping to record something terrible happening.

And so -

And so when the Nevises came out and said please help, our daughter has been carried away by the flooding, we saw a dozen cameras and a dozen bloggers and a dozen reporters turn their attention on this one story that, unfortunately for them, turned out to be, as we all learned later, completely false.

And this is one of the things you talk about in the new book, that the current model of the news media makes this kind of false, um, or I guess we would call it mistaken reporting a, uh, a more... well would make it more likely to occur.

That's exactly the point I tried to make in the book, that without a gap between a news event occurring and a newsperson reporting it we leave ourselves open to all sorts of, uh, all sorts of problems.

There are people who say, So what? So what if the news reported right at the moment that something happens is wrong? The true story always comes out eventually. So what if we all think the wrong thing for a couple of days?

Well I think that the people who say that have a, uh, a higher opinion of people's intellect than I do. I would point to, I mean there are many examples I give a number of examples in the book of people whose careers have been ruined by public prejudice against them for what in the end turns out to be misreported facts. Um. And it's just a matter of the press needing, uh, needing to provide the most sensational stories to wrestle viewers away from the other networks, where their reporters are working to provide the most sensational stories.

But isn't that just good TV? Some people would argue that that's what keeps the news game sharp, pushes them to be up-to-the-minute.

Look it would be one thing if this was a matter of, as I say several times in the book, a news culture like the one that existed when I was a kid, where you basically had two anchors on for one hour every night. That gave the producers and the reporters plenty of time to construct compelling, insightful, um, hard-hitting news copy and still vet their facts. Nowadays you have people basically inventing the content on the ground and on the scene, and it's inevitable that sooner or later the need for sensationalism is going to outweigh the need for journalistic, um, journalistic I guess integrity or maybe standards is a better word.

You talk a lot in this book about the Nevis family, those people who told the authorities that their daughter had been carried off by the floodwaters. We haven't heard much about them lately. What happened to them? I understand you, uh, you spoke with them quite extensively for the book have you spoken with them lately?

Uh, no I haven't spoke with them lately. I met Frank, I met Frank on this show actually, when I was on this show a little less than a year ago and the fellow sitting in for you that night was gracious enough to invite me back when this book was finished... Uh, I met Frank and actually spoke with him and his wife Victoria several times throughout the course of writing this book... Frank is an interesting case or I should say Frank and Victoria are an interesting case because... Let's see if I can remember how I said it to them... The way I see it is that Frank and Victoria understood intuitively what I understood academically about the flaws in the new media environment in which we're living. Their story, and it's a really fascinating story, and I tell it in the book, is the story of two people who make all the right moves and who do it pretty much on their own - they did hire a public relations firm toward the end of their saga but for the most part these people staged what was in effect a full-scale guerilla assault on American celebrity. I mean not against American celebrity but to achieve and attain celebrity. And it started with an exploitation of this phenomenon, this glitch in the system that made it so they could basically crash into the public consciousness.

What was the, uh, what was the main goal?

Um, if you ask Frank and Victoria that question they'll tell you that the goal was to get their reality show back into production, this reality show they very briefly at one point were in talks with a network to make.. Um, I think that if you asked them that's what they would tell you but after talking with them and watching them I think the TV show, the reality show, and by the way I'm sure your viewers will remember that they did succeed in resurrecting the show...

I was going to say I think I remember something about that.

...Right they managed to resurrect the show, uh, briefly resurrect the show, I think it ended up running for something like a half-dozen episodes and I think they ended up only being aired online.

So the show's kaput, so then what happens? Do they manage to, uh, I guess stay famous or have they basically ended up back where they started?

Well during the whole course of this they moved to L.A. and so at the very least they're not back where they started per se... Uh, I know that about a month after production of the show stopped they dissolved their contract with their PR company and the last time I talked to Frank, this was maybe a three months ago, pretty much right before the book came out he told me that he was talking to some people at one of the networks about being a guest host on a game show, the regular host is retiring and they're looking for someone to fill in until they can get a full time replacement so I guess he's talking to them about that... Uh, you know how you never know about these things, that could end up being something or it could end up being nothing. And then Victoria is actually working on a cookbook for Young and Reed... Which is actually owned by Victor and Straub, who published my book so who knows, maybe we'll end up bumping into each other in the hallway sometime. I think it's some sort of tie-in with the reality show, a cookbook for cooking for a big family, something like that.

So we wouldn't say that they, that they didn't succeed in their efforts.

Oh no not by any stretch. I mean are they A-listers? Certainly not. But they're out here. They're in the conversation.

Incredible.

Customer Reviews for the title: **MediaFrenzy: How the New Media Feeding Frenzy is Destroying America** by Dr. David Sellers

"Interesting and Insightful" by Lionel Peters (Charlotte, NC)
Star Rating: 5/5
2 of 20 people found this review helpful.

Dr. David Sellers has written a very interesting book. In it he says that the way that the news media reports the news these days makes it easy for people to make mistakes and misreport the facts. He gives a lot of examples and shows how more careful practices could solve the problem. I thought his writing style was very clear and the things he had to say were very interesting. From the author bio it says that he is a professor of media studies and you can tell that he really knows what he is talking about. Great book!

Help other readers find the most helpful reviews.
Was this review helpful to you? Yes No

"Aren't we done with this yet?" by Steven Saunders (Portland, ME)
Star Rating: 5/5
14 of 20 people found this review helpful.

My media studies professor was a student of Dr. Sellers when he was in college and he made us read this book for our intro to media studies class. The book is pretty interesting, and Sellers makes a lot of insightful points and uses a lot of good examples to back up what he's saying. I gave the book five out of five stars because the book is really well put together. My problem with the book doesn't have anything to do with the book itself. Maybe it's just that I had to read it for school, but I didn't find myself all that interested in this material. Sellers works really hard to establish that it's a really big problem when people get the wrong news, that it has all of these real-world repercussions... maybe it's a generational thing, but I don't feel like whenever I hear something I start to go crazy about it. I mean I know that some people do, but I feel like me and people my age (I'm 21) are used to things being thrown at us... Honestly I don't even watch the news because i know that sooner or later if something is a really big deal it's going to find its way to me. Sellers makes a big point about how there are so many avenues for the news to travel, but he doesn't even mention that all of those channels have a way of filtering out anything that isn't important or verifiable. He is adamant that it's a bad thing that everything gets put out onto the news networks or the internet immediately without considering that that might actually put the news under *more* scrutiny, not less. Fifty years ago people trusted what they read and saw on TV because they assumed the reporters had checked their facts... now everybody knows that they should wait to form an opinion. The other thing that kind of drove me a little bit nuts about this book is that Sellers' main example through pretty much the whole thing is Melissa Nevis, the "Gill Falls Girl," whose parents told everybody that she got carried over a waterfall and it became a big news frenzy. The thing he only briefly touches on is that Melissa was missing for 9 DAYS... definitely long enough for the story to become a news frenzy whether it was reported right away or not. Sellers keeps using it as an example of how easily the current news media can be deceived, without ever admitting the point that if it worked now it would have worked during the days of his vaunted "desk and anchor." After all: 9 days is plenty of time to check the facts. The other point he keeps making is how dire the repercussions of these kind of mistakes are... He does use a number of good examples of how people's lives have been altered by mistakes in reporting, but he always comes back to Melissa Nevis as the shining example of what happens when reporting goes wrong. Honestly, it took us all a minute in class to even remember what he was talking about. Who remembers these things? That's the big problem with Sellers' logic: he wants to make a case that once something is reported it becomes permanent and that's why it's problematic, but he doesn't have to look far to find a million examples of times when something that gets reported gets forgotten the minute it's said, and the exact opposite thing can be said the next day. That's the bigger issue with the "mediafrenzy": we're all so used to hearing so much stuff all the time that we don't even bother paying attention, much less remembering. I mean really: who still cares about Melissa Nevis?

ADAM BLACK lives and works in Cleveland, Ohio. *THE PRANK* is his first novel.

www.ingramcontent.com/pod-product-compliance
Lightning Source LLC
Chambersburg PA
CBHW050021180626

46810CB00002B/523